HOW TO BE A
HERO

For Georgia and Immie,
even though you stole all my pens.

First published 2021 by Macmillan Children's Books
a division of Macmillan Publishers Limited
The Smithson, 6 Briset Street, London EC1M 5NR
Basingstoke and Oxford
Associated companies throughout the world
www.panmacmillan.com

ISBN 978-1-5290-4503-1

Text copyright © Cat Weldon 2021
Illustrations copyright © Katie Kear 2021

The right of Cat Weldon and Katie Kear to be identified as the author
and illustrator of this work has been asserted by them in accordance
with the Copyright, Designs and Patents Act 1988.

1 3 5 7 9 8 6 4 2

A CIP catalogue record for this book is available from the British Library.

Printed and bound by CPI Group (UK) Ltd, Croydon CR0 4YY

·HOW TO BE A· HERO

CAT WELDON

Illustrated by Kate Kear

MACMILLAN CHILDREN'S BOOKS

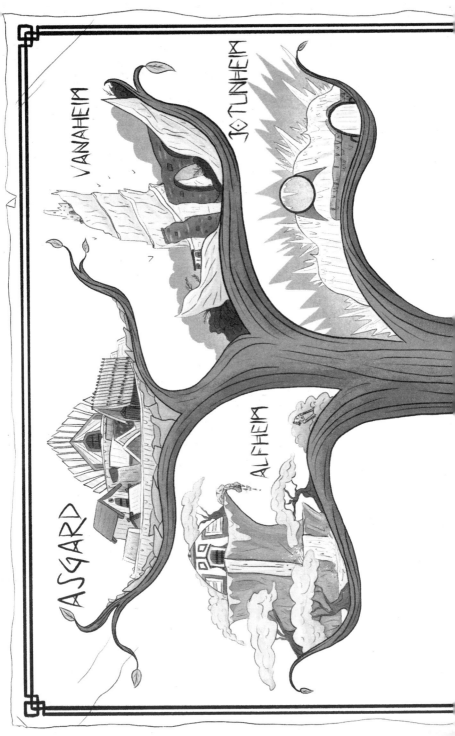

MIDGARD

SHATTERBONE MINE

SILENT SHIVER FOREST

THIEVES' CAMP

KRUD

GREAT HALL OF KRUD

BJØRN'S WHIFFY BOG

COAST OF SHRIEKS

Chapter One

The Cup of Krud

'TONIGHT WE FEAST – TOMORROW WE FIGHT!' The enormous man, big enough to be two normal men but average-sized for one Viking, raised his drinking horn high into the air. Ale slopped out of it and rained down on those sitting around the rough wooden table.

Another man raised his hand. 'Erm, who are we fighting? Because we're not *technically* at war with anybody right now.'

The enormous man paused, his red face screwed up in thought.

'How about, *Tonight we feast – tomorrow we go on a nice picnic?*' the other Viking continued, mopping ale off his head with his sleeve. 'I like picnics.'

'No – it's supposed to rain tomorrow,' replied one with tufty hair tied back in pigtails. 'What about, *Tonight we feast – tomorrow we pick our toenails?*'

'Or, *Tonight we feast – tomorrow we press flowers?*'

'Ha, after eating Ethel's cooking it should be, *Tonight we feast – tomorrow we have toxic turnip breath,*' croaked a voice from the back. Several people grumbled in agreement, then

1

ducked as Ethel threw a ladle across the room.

A Viking with a dark, brushy beard climbed ponderously to his feet and silenced the room with a loud burp. '*Tonight we feast – tomorrow . . . we have an Ultimate Shin-Kicking Contest!*'

This suggestion received an enormous cheer. The air filled with ale foam and half-chewed food as cups and plates were tossed towards the rafters.

Unnoticed by anyone, a pale, scruffy boy put down the tray he carried and ducked out of the door. The boy's name was Whetstone. It wasn't a very good name and he didn't like it much, but it was all he had.

Outside, the cool air tickled his white skin, making the hairs on his arms rise. Whetstone pulled his thin cloak around his shoulders and stepped away from the door. Cutting through the wispy clouds above him hung a bright yellow moon, giving him just enough light to see by.

Behind him in the Great Hall of Krud, the Vikings were still cheering. Whetstone had only been in the village for a couple of days, having managed to blag a job in the kitchens. It hadn't been hard – there wasn't exactly a queue to help clean up after Viking feasts, and trying to get grease stains off the ceiling was a NIGHTMARE. All Vikings were the same – finding any excuse to guzzle and gorge all night until their already pink, blotchy faces grew pinker and blotchier, and they all fell asleep under the table. Whetstone gazed up at the moon and grinned. They wouldn't be celebrating when they found out what his real plans were.

A deathly-white hand dropped on to Whetstone's shoulder and his heart jumped into his mouth as he spun around. 'Oh, Vali! It's you.' He sagged with relief.

The taller boy nodded at him. 'Come on – you know he doesn't like being kept waiting.' He released Whetstone and headed away from the Great Hall, finding his way easily in the darkness.

'I couldn't get out earlier.' Whetstone skipped after him.

'I'm supposed to be working at the feast. I saw the cup though.'

Vali grabbed hold of Whetstone's tunic. In his free hand, a knife gleamed. 'I know Light Finger thinks you're the one who's going to take it, but remember – I was here first.' He gave Whetstone a little shake. 'You're a nobody. We felt sorry for you, that was all.' The boy released Whetstone's tunic. 'Once you have the cup, you give it to me. Understand?'

Whetstone brushed himself off. It was impossible to imagine that Vali – this boy with dark, sunken eyes and almost translucent skin – had been the one to convince him to leave home and join the thieves. It seemed unimaginable that he had been nice once.

With a final look behind him, Vali led the way out of the village and moved towards a nearby thicket of trees. A flickering light appeared – it was the thieves' camp. Whetstone followed Vali towards the firelight, tripping as his too-large boots caught in unseen rabbit holes and clumps of rough grass.

They stepped into the circle of light. A shabby-looking man with overly large front teeth glanced up. The long wooden staff he used to support a damaged leg lay by his side.

'Did you see it, on the shelf next to the fireplace? Chief Awfulrick always likes to display his treasures during feasts.' The man spat into the fire, which spluttered green for a moment.

Whetstone nodded slowly, thinking of the golden cup studded with jewels he had seen while collecting plates. 'Light Finger, are you sure it has to be *me* that steals it?'

'I'm doing this as a *favour* to you, Whetstone. Don't you

want Fortune and Glory?' the ratty-looking man probed. 'Or would you rather scrub porridge out of pans for the rest of your life?'

Vali dropped on to a nearby tree stump and sniggered. 'Yeah, you might as well get used to thieving. It's not as though you're going to turn out to be a Hero, are you?'

'Watch out, Vali. If you carry on like that, Whetstone will think you don't like him.'

Vali gave Whetstone a pained smile, the blade still in his hand, twisting easily through his fingers.

Whetstone shifted awkwardly, his eyes fixed on the knife.

'It's not the boy's fault you failed to get the cup,' Light Finger snarled. He turned back to Whetstone. 'You're not going to fail me, are you, Whetstone? I know this is your first big theft, and it's natural to feel nervous, but you'll soon get used to it.'

'He hasn't got the guts for it,' Vali scoffed, picking at his nails with the dagger. 'Let me have another try. It's only a cup, after all.'

'No!' Light Finger snapped. 'You had your chance. This is Whetstone's job now. It's taken me years to track down that cup, and I'm not leaving Krud without it.'

Vali stabbed the knife into the tree stump and leaned back on his arms, his expression hidden in shadows.

'It's only a shame I can't take it myself. Alas, I am too recognizable, too well known, too—'

'Slow?' Vali dodged a blow from Light Finger's staff.

Whetstone dug his nails into his palms. 'If I take it, you're sure I'll be famous?'

The man nodded. 'More than your wildest dreams.'

Whetstone sighed. He had some pretty wild dreams. In his heart he knew he didn't have the skills to be a great warrior – he could hardly lift a sword and preferred running away to fighting. He would never make it as an explorer due to chronic seasickness. But a thief? . . . *That* was a possibility. He was quick and sneaky and no one seemed to notice him much.

When Vali and Light Finger, the Greatest Thief in All the Known World, had arrived in his village, and Vali suggested Whetstone join them, it had seemed too good an opportunity to miss. People loved telling stories of Light Finger's exploits. If Whetstone could steal great treasures just like Light Finger, then people would know his name and sing stories about his fantastic adventures too. Then he would be *somebody*. And being somebody, even a thief, was better than being nobody. All he had to do was steal Awfulrick's stupid cup, and then he could be part of the thieves' gang for good.

'Mind you, the life of a celebrity isn't everything it's

cracked up to be . . .' Light Finger sighed. 'All the autograph signing and people trying to kiss you. You're just a kid – you don't want to be worried about that.'

Whetstone felt his cheeks burn.

'You'll never get a minute's rest. Everywhere you go it will be, *Whetstone, tell us about the time you* . . . Well, never mind that. You haven't actually done anything yet, *have you?*'

The boy bit his lip. The thought of returning home to the village of Drott as Whetstone the Sly, or Whetstone the Cunning, anything instead of Whetstone the Nothing, made his head buzz. But at the same time he felt bad about stealing from Awfulrick and the Vikings of Krud. They had been quite kind to him, really. He hadn't even had too many chicken bones thrown at him during the feast.

Light Finger seemed to sense Whetstone's doubts. Using his staff to lever himself upright, the crooked man got to his feet. He loomed over Whetstone, who was treated to a lovely view right up his nose. A large, knobbly bogey hung there, glinting in the moonlight. He wrapped his arm around Whetstone's shoulder.

'I've been keeping an eye on you, Whetstone, whenever I dropped into Drott over the years.' Light Finger smiled. 'I knew you were going to be very useful to me one day.'

Vali tossed something into the fire behind them; the flames fizzled.

Whetstone remembered his life in the cold, grey village of Drott and shuddered. He had lived there with his foster mother, Angrboda (or the Angry Bogey, as he secretly called her), in her rescue home for orphaned wolf cubs, Dunhowlin'. She had taken him in after he turned up suddenly in the middle of the village in a basket. No one knew where he really came from.

'I still think it's a mistake,' Vali said from the shadows. 'The runt will only mess it up.'

Light Finger snarled, his ratty teeth casting odd shadows on his face. 'Be quiet, you.'

He turned back to Whetstone. 'Vali doesn't understand. He's not like us. The cup is the key.'

Light Finger often said that.

'The key to what, though?'

'To you joining us, of course!' he said quickly. 'Don't you want a place to belong?' He gave Whetstone's shoulder another squeeze. 'Remember what I told you: the cup is magical. It can tell us many things. Things that will make us famous.'

'Us?'

'You, of course. *The Saga of Whetstone and the Magic Cup* – I can hear it already.'

Whetstone narrowed his eyes. Light Finger was desperate to get his hands on Awfulrick's cup; it was all he talked about. He claimed it could tell fortunes. 'I still don't understand why you picked me to do this.'

'Call it my Master Thief instincts. That cup will unlock an amazing future for you, but first you have to *hold it in your hands*. I don't take just anyone on as my apprentice, you know. After all, I am—'

'*The Greatest Thief in All the Known World*,' Whetstone

recited. Light Finger squeezed his shoulder again, his grip painfully tight.

'I know, I know,' the boy muttered.

'I have taken the jewelled crown of Queen Helga of the Ironfists,' Light Finger continued, his eyes bright with past victories. 'Plundered the famed pearl of the Merpeople, and . . .'

'. . . and picked the pockets of kings, queens and princes,' Whetstone finished. He liked hearing these stories, almost as much as Light Finger liked telling them.

'My thefts are a way of adding a little spice to the boring run of days. What is life without a twist or turn along the way?'

Whetstone's fingers wound the edge of his cloak into knots. 'Don't you ever worry about getting caught?'

Vikings were not kind to thieves. If Awfulrick caught him, Whetstone would probably be marooned on the Barren Islands to be eaten by the wild beasts who lived there. Or maybe Awfulrick would force-feed him mouldy toenails until he choked. Or worst of all, perhaps Whetstone would have to hand-wash the skid marks out of all the Viking underpants in the village. Fame and Fortune were all very well, but you had to be alive to enjoy them.

Light Finger released the boy's shoulder and moved away. 'Maybe Vali's right. Maybe you're not brave enough.' He scratched his stubbly chin with the top of his staff. The silvery snakes that decorated it sparkled in the moonlight. 'I suppose I'll just have to take you back to Drott.'

'No way. I'm not going back,' Whetstone said stoutly. If the price of leaving the Angry Bogey was taking Awfulrick's cup, well, Awfulrick would just have to get another one. 'I'll get the cup – and the glory too.'

'Excellent!' Light Finger clapped him on the shoulder. His mouth curved into a cold smile. 'Like Vali said, it's only a cup. Then it's off to the great city of Cloggibum, and minstrels will be—'

'Singing songs about us before nightfall?'

❀

Watching Whetstone pick his way through the darkness back to the Great Hall, Light Finger turned to the older boy. 'You should go after him. Keep an eye on our dear little orphan. We can't afford any mistakes now – not when we're so close.'

Vali spat into the long grass at his feet.

Light Finger grabbed him by the arm and peered into the boy's face. 'Only a few days more. Twelve years of planning just for this moment; soon I'll have all the power I ever dreamed of. The boy gets us the cup; the cup gets us the riddle—'

'And when we've got the riddle, we won't need the boy any more.'

Light Finger released Vali and smiled. 'Something like that.'

❀

The Vikings of Krud were still feasting. Whetstone followed the sound of crashing, smashing and out-of-tune singing towards the Great Hall. Viking feasts were legendary. And very, very messy. They would be eating big lumps of meat, carousing (which is like singing but involves trying to drown the person next to you with your drink), throwing axes, and, if they were very unlucky, there might even be poetry.

Whetstone pushed open the door to the Great Hall. The smell of sweaty men and women poured out – it was like being slapped in the face with a piece of warm ham. Whetstone held his breath and sidled inside. Luckily no one seemed to have noticed he'd disappeared.

A group of large men, each the shape of an upside-down triangle (this was the proper shape for a Viking: massive, wide shoulders, arms like tree trunks, and legs like twigs, with round heads the size of pumpkins), were clustered together singing. In the centre of the group, stuffing a whole sheep's leg in his mouth, stood Awfulrick, Chief of Krud. Whetstone wiped his suddenly sweaty hands on his tunic and scooped up some plates.

> *Oh the third day is Odin's day,*
> *God of wisdom, song and war,*

the Vikings warbled,

> *On this day we drink and feast*
> *Until our tums get sore!*

Whetstone pulled up his hood to muffle the singing and ducked to avoid a thrown goblet. They might be loud, they might be enthusiastic, but they were not in tune.

Oh the fourth day is Thor's day,

Awfulrick and the Vikings sang on,

> *God of storms and lightning,*
> *We think he is a really great guy*
> *Who gives the Giants a . . . pounding!*

Whetstone winced at the dodgy rhymes and tried to focus on the cup. Pretending to scrape something sticky off one of the plates with a blunt knife, he straightened up and leaned away from the table. Behind Awfulrick was the fireplace. Next to the fireplace was the shelf. On the shelf, reflecting leaping flames, was the golden cup Light Finger wanted so badly. Its coloured jewels sparkled, making rainbows dance along the rough wooden timbers of the hall.

Whetstone stared at it, hypnotized by the bright colours. A chicken bone smacked into his ear, making him drop the plate and knife. He sank to his knees and scuttled under the table after them.

> *Oh the fifth day is Frigg's day,*
> *Goddess of fam-i-lee!*

She knows the fates of mortal men,
Just like you and meeeee!

Awfulrick finished in a very squeaky solo, his walrus-skin boots lifting on to tiptoe as he struggled to hit the high notes.

Asgard! Asgard!
Home of Gods and fun,
Asgard! Asgard!
Until the Frost Giants come.

As the Vikings chanted the chorus, Whetstone abandoned the dirty plate and knife to crawl closer to Awfulrick and the cup.

Valhalla! Valhalla!
The place where Heroes go,
Valhalla! Valhalla!
When they're slain by their foe!

The song reached its table-thumping crescendo. A nearby bench crashed to the floor, bringing a crowd of Vikings tumbling down in a sweaty, tangled heap. The noise made Whetstone jump, banging his head on the underside of a table. Stars danced in front of his eyes. The Vikings cheered and whooped.

Rubbing his aching head, he climbed out from beneath the table. *Now, while everyone's distracted – it has to be now.*

Hearing a whirring noise, Whetstone ducked. A flying axe

embedded itself into the wall just above his head, showering him in plaster. Gulping, he fixed his eyes on the cup. There it was, glinting in the firelight, just out of reach. His fingers itched at the thought of touching it. *I CAN do this! There is no WAY I'm going back to the Angry Bogey*, he told himself, edging towards the fireplace.

A large cauldron suspended by thin chains hung above the fire. The smell made Whetstone's mouth water. An old lady with an alarming amount of ear hair stood stirring the pot. 'You look like you could use feeding up, lad,' she croaked, pushing a bowl into his hands. The smell hit his nostrils like a hammer, making his stomach clench.

'It's got sheep eyeballs in it.' She held out a ladle. A milky-white eyeball floated to the surface. 'Good for you – helps you see in the dark.' She poured it, eyeball and all, into his bowl. The eyeball stared at him. Whetstone stared back at it and shuddered.

Someone knocked into Whetstone's shoulder. The stew slopped in his bowl, making the eyeball sink down under the filmy water. Whetstone turned to find a handsome youth with a highly polished helmet standing behind him. The youth sniggered and brushed his gleaming red hair out of his face.

'What do you think you're doing, Weasel-from-the-Kitchens?' he asked with a sneer. 'This section is for VIVs only.'

'VIVs?'

'Very Important Vikings.'

'What are you doing here then, Bragi?' called a loud voice. The owner looked like he ate live puffins for breakfast. It was the man with the dark, brushy beard who had suggested the Ultimate Shin-Kicking Contest. Whetstone gulped. Bragi scowled. The bearded man laughed and clapped Bragi on the shoulder, making his helmet slip down over his eyes and come to rest on his large nose. Whetstone tried not to giggle.

'I'm keeping an eye on this cockroach, Oresmiter.' Bragi pushed his helmet back into place. 'Just because Awfulrick gave him a job, it doesn't mean we should trust him.' Bragi looked down his long nose at the scruffy boy. 'He's not from Krud. Maybe I should throw him on to the dungheap, just in case?'

'Don't be a prat, Bragi. What happened to Viking hospitality? You never know who might be knocking on your door.' Oresmiter scrutinized Whetstone from under thick eyebrows. 'But why *are* you hanging about up here?'

'He's certainly not eating!' called the hag by the cauldron.

15

'And I shaved the trotters before I put them in.'

Whetstone felt more and more eyes turn to look at him. His face started to burn. 'I was—' he stumbled. 'I was only—' With a clang, his bowl dropped to the floor through trembling fingers, the eyeball rolling between Bragi's feet and staring at him balefully.

Oresmiter rested his hand on the axe that hung from his belt. 'Yes?'

Whetstone trailed to a stop. Usually he didn't have any trouble finding the right words, but now he couldn't think of a single one. A prickle of sweat broke out between his shoulder blades.

'I was only c-coming to tell you that you forgot the verse about Tyr. In your song, you forgot the God of Justice.' The lie popped out just in time.

Oresmiter peered into Whetstone's face, who tried to smile winningly, but his dry lips got stuck to his teeth.

Oresmiter's face cleared. 'By Odin's eyebrows, he's right!' he yelled. 'Oi, Awfulrick – we forgot about Tyr!'

He turned to them, his face red from the heat of the fire. He glowered at a wide-eyed Whetstone, then slapped himself on the forehead, making his helmet ring. 'GREAT THOR'S TOENAILS, HOW COULD WE FORGET ABOUT TYR? HE'S MY FAVOURITE!'

A large meaty hand reached out and yanked Whetstone into the group of singing Vikings. Whetstone found himself surrounded by a collection of massive hairy men. He thought he could smell bacon.

Awfulrick clamped Whetstone under his armpit. 'ALL TOGETHER NOW!' The boy held his breath to avoid the wafts of Awfulrick's body odour.

Oh the second day is Tyr's day,

the Viking choir began, swaying in time to the song.

Despite almost being dragged off his feet by the rocking Vikings, the boy felt a jolt of excitement. The cup sat directly behind him.

Lord of rules and law . . .

Trying to only move one arm, Whetstone reached out behind him. The wooden shelf containing the cup appeared under his fingers. He quickly ran his hand along the rough plank.

He had his hand bitten clean off . . .

Whetstone's arm twisted, his fingers stretching out, desperately hoping to find something that wasn't made of splinters. He gritted his teeth, his elbow feeling like it was going to pop. But then his fingertips brushed against something smooth and cool. The cup! Whetstone wiggled his fingers, nudging the cup into his palm. He closed his hand around it. With a faint metallic rasp, Whetstone pulled his arm back and the cup disappeared into his cloak pocket.

Which must have made it sore!

The Viking choir exploded into the chorus once more, and Whetstone tried to sing along, his heart hammering in his chest.

> *Asgard! Asgard!*
> *Home of Gods and fun,*
> *Asgard! Asgard!*
> *Until the Frost Giants come.*

Whetstone leaned away as Awfulrick's bearskin waistcoat tickled him under the nose. He had done it. He had stolen the jewelled cup. Now he just had to get away with it.

Chapter Two

This Is Your
ULTIMATE PURPOSE

Far above Whetstone and the Vikings of Krud, a girl unfolded a crumpled booklet and flattened it out. Her forehead wrinkled as she read:

A Guide to the Nine Worlds
By Blood-Runs-Cold, Leader of the Valkyries

The Nine Worlds

Imagine the biggest tree you can. No, bigger than that.
BIGGER.
BIGGER.
That's Yggdrasil, and it makes your tree look like a bit of wilted broccoli. Nine whole worlds hang from Yggdrasil, *that's* how big it is.

Asgard: Right at the top, because it's the best. Home of the Gods and ruled over by Odin. In Asgard you can find

Valhalla, Odin's Great Hall, where the greatest warriors come after they've died. There they can fight, feast and drink until *Ragnarok*, the battle at the end of the world. At Ragnarok they will be called upon to fight the Frost Giants for Odin, but until then it's basically party time.

Vanaheim: Home to the Gods who aren't cool enough to be in Asgard. They're mostly interested in growing stuff; inhabitants of Asgard are more interested in fighting.

Alfheim: Home of the Elves. Yes, they have pointy ears. Yes, they giggle a lot. Mostly harmless, but keep them where you can see them.

Jotunheim: Home of the Giants, including our mortal enemies the Frost Giants. They keep trying to break into Asgard; we keep beating them in battle. Lots of mountains; good for skiing.

Midgard: This is where you can find living humans, living their ordinary lives, with ordinary horses, ordinary farms and ordinary families.

Svartalfheim: Home of the Dwarves. A maze of caves and mines. They love tinkering with gold and making magical gadgets.

Muspell: Land of Fire. Ruled over by Sutr, a Fire Giant. Nice saunas.

Helheim: Home of the Queen of the Dead, Hel. Yes, she named the place after herself. Tells you everything you need to know, really.

Niflheim: Land of the Unworthy Dead. The dragon Nidhogg lives here and chews on the roots of the world tree. He likes poetry, gold and trampling anyone unlucky enough to be sent there.

Who's Who in Asgard

Odin: The Allfather, the Spear Shaker, the Terrifying One-Eyed Chief of the Gods. The boss.

Frigg: Goddess of Family. Odin's wife. Knows the future but won't tell anyone.

Loki: The Trickster. Enjoys a 'joke'. Approach with caution. Technically a Fire Giant, but Odin lets him live in Asgard because they're blood brothers.

Thor: God of Thunder. Do not touch his hammer. Seriously.

Freyja: Goddess of Love and Sorcery. Likes cats.

The Valkyries: Elite female warriors, Valkyries are created by Odin, Chief of the Gods. Their main job is to bring the greatest warriors and Heroes to Valhalla on their flying horses. At Ragnarok, the battle at the end of the world, they will lead the Gods and warriors of Valhalla in the final clash against the Frost Giants.

Travel between Worlds

It is possible to travel between worlds by flying or climbing through Yggdrasil's branches. Not easy, but possible. Only the Gods (and Valkyries) have really got the hang of it. The Giants have managed it a few times, more through luck than anything else.

Valkyries and Odin travel by flying horse, Loki has special shoes, and Freyja uses a magic cloak. The Bifrost Bridge links Asgard and Midgard. When humans on Midgard see it, they call it a rainbow.

Magic

It's simple: magic can only be created by magical creatures– Dwarves, Elves, and to a certain extent, Giants. All other magic comes from magical objects *made* by magical creatures, usually the Dwarves.

Except for Odin: he learned how to do magic by hanging upside down from Yggdrasil for nine days to discover the secrets of the runes. Fancy doing that? No? Then no magic for you.

Lotta folded the much-creased booklet and stuffed it under the leather bands of her wrist guards next to her brown skin. Lotta was a trainee Valkyrie, and today was going to be their first trip to collect fallen warriors from Midgard, so she didn't want to make any mistakes.

'I can do this,' she muttered, jamming a metal helmet on top of her dark curls and dodging through the narrow archway. 'It's easy. Midgard is down. Asgard is up.'

She ducked to avoid a wonky wooden sign. Just readable through arrow holes and sword gouges were the words:

Beyond the archway, a ragtag group of girls prepared their horses for a journey. They might be dressed in identical armour, but that was the only matching thing about them. Valkyries were born out of Viking battles across Midgard, and their appearance depended on where they had been created.

Each of the trainees wore a breastplate of overlapping leather and metal strips, with a linen shirt and heavy, pleated skirt. Thick bands of leather protected their forearms, and heavy boots with metal studs covered their feet. Lotta paused to pull her hairy socks up – they kept slipping down inside her boots and getting stuck under her feet.

A pair of bored-looking looking Class Two Valkyries were supposed to be supervising the trainees. A tall black girl with elbow-length dreadlocks was speaking loudly to her friend, a girl with freckles scattered across her pink-cheeked face. 'D'you remember when we went on our first trip to Midgard? I got seventy-eight per cent on my Collecting Fallen Warriors score for getting Jarl the Jelly-Jowls back to Valhalla in one piece.'

The pink-cheeked girl rolled her eyes. 'Whatever, Akrid.'

Lotta pulled her helmet firmly down over her ears. She was nervous enough without the older Valkyries making her feel worse.

She scuttled over to her horse and fastened a bridle around its head. Tight black curls escaped from under her helmet and brushed her neck. Her horse tried to take a bite out of them. Lotta jerked out of the way of his yellow teeth and scowled.

'Thor's beard! Are you trying to look scary, Lotta?' called a sarcastic voice.

Lotta turned to see a girl with long silver plaits and pale skin climbing on to her own horse. It stamped on the flagstones, hooves sending up blue sparks.

'You look like you're desperate for a wee!' the girl, Flay, said with a laugh.

A girl with identical plaits and an identical gleeful look on her face sniggered. This was Flee, Flay's twin sister.

Lotta carefully avoided looking at the twins and focused instead on swinging herself up into her saddle. Feeling embarrassed was not very Valkyrie-like, but then, neither was Lotta.

There were three classes of Valkyrie. Class Ones were full Valkyries who went out on the most important missions. They swooped low over Viking battlefields, inspiring the fighting with their bloodcurdling cries. Class Twos were Valkyries who had almost finished their training; they were often used to send messages from the Gods to the rest of the Nine Worlds, or to inspire minstrels to write great stories about Heroes and famous battles. Then there were Class Threes: they were the trainees and rarely got to do anything more exciting than practising their axe-throwing or reciting petrifying poetry. Most Valkyries started training when they were around eleven years old and would be Class Ones when they reached eighteen. Lotta had already been in the training school for over a year and was not doing well.

Lotta jiggled her horse's reins, intending to move away from the sisters and into the wide courtyard. Her horse had other ideas.

'No, Thighbiter. Stop it.' Lotta hauled on the reins as he twisted around, trying to bite her on the leg. He was always doing that. Thighbiter jerked sideways, clonking Lotta's head on the low-hanging sign.

'Ow!' Lotta tried to grab the sign as it swung back, the words *Valkyrie Training School* looming before smacking her between the eyes. Lotta pulled off her helmet and rubbed at her forehead. Akrid, the Class Two Valkyrie with dreadlocks, sighed and crossed her arms.

VALKYRIE
TRAINING SCHOOL
BE THE BEST IN THE BATTLE
AGAINST THE FROST GIANTS

'You might as well get used to it, barnacle breath,' Flay called from her horse as they trotted past. 'You're going to be stuck as a Class Three Valkyrie for a very looooong time.'

Lotta shoved the sign away and wedged her helmet back on top of her curls, trying to pull it low over her face. Flay might be saying what everyone else was thinking, but Lotta was determined to prove them wrong. In order to become full Valkyries, the trainees were supposed to show their mastery of six key skills. The current level of Valkyrieness of each trainee was shown on the circular shields they carried, which were split into segments – one for each skill. The segments glowed according to how well the trainee was doing in that particular element.

Someone like Flay or Flee had a shield that glowed brightly in most of the segments. Lotta's shield, on the other hand, wasn't very bright at all, and several of the segments were almost dark, miles away from the sixty per cent she needed in each section to move up to being a Class Two.

'Ahem.'

Valkyrie Training School Report

Name: Brings-A-Lot-Of-Scrapes-And-Grazes (Lotta)

Class: Third

Skill

Fighting: 35 %

Axes should be thrown FORWARD, Lotta!

Good at polishing armour though.

Horse Riding: 30 %

Is distrusted by the horses.

Was chucked into a bush last week.

Epic Poetry: 28 %

Let's just not mention your version

of the *Saga of Svenson the Selfish*.

Transforming into Swans: 38 %

Looks more like a duck. Keeps questioning

why it has to be a swan – it just does, Lotta!

Serving Mead in Valhalla: 53 %

Not bad, but it is pretty easy.

Collecting Fallen Warriors: 0 %

First battle visit next week – please don't mess it up.

Overall Hero Score: 31 %

Signed: *Blood-Runs-Cold*, Leader of the Valkyries

The girls spun around in their saddles to see a heavily armoured shadow squinting at them from the stable doorway. Leading her own massive warhorse, Blood-Runs-Cold – or Scold, as she was known to the trainees – stepped into the courtyard. The Class Two Valkyries snapped to attention.

Scold was a statuesque woman with olive skin and powerful lungs. Legend said she once cleared an entire battlefield with one enormous sneeze; among her other jobs she was responsible for training the Class Threes.

Scold swung herself up on to her horse, Thunder Trumper. She turned to the assorted bunch of girl warriors. 'I'm sure I don't have to remind you of how important today is,' Scold roared. 'Each of you was created from pure battle frenzy, brought to life by the breath of Odin. We may each come from separate places in Midgard, but we are united in one ULTIMATE PURPOSE: serving Odin by bringing back fallen warriors to fill Valhalla!' She jabbed a finger in the direction of a huge wooden building behind them. It might not

seem much from the outside, but being picked to spend your afterlife in Valhalla was a Viking's idea of paradise.

Being in Valhalla was quite a good set-up, really. The fallen warriors were magically restored by Odin and spent their days on the field beside the hall, practising their biting, kicking, gouging and sword-fighting ready to support Odin when the Frost Giants invaded. Then all evening in the Great Hall, partying.

Scold took a deep breath. 'I have done all I can to prepare you. We have practised flying in formation, we have rehearsed how to get mighty warriors on to your horses without hurting yourselves.'

'Lift with your knees,' Lotta muttered.

'You have been tested on selecting the best warriors out of the bunch. Today is a chance to PROVE YOURSELVES ONCE AND FOR ALL!' Her voice boomed around the empty courtyard, making a pile of abandoned helmets ring metallically.

'I believe some of you are more ready for this responsibility than others,' Scold continued, definitely *not* looking at Lotta. 'Needless to say, if you do well, you could all be on the way to becoming CLASS TWO VALKYRIES!'

A short trainee with an intense expression squeaked with excitement.

Flee raised her hand. 'Please, Scold, what happens if we don't bring a warrior back?'

Flay giggled and looked at Lotta.

Scold scowled as she stuck a spikey helmet on her head.

'Just bring one back, OK? It's pretty basic stuff. If you can't master this, well, then you can't be a Valkyrie. Not even a Class Three.'

Scold's eyes lingered on Lotta a moment. The girl puffed up her chest and pushed her shoulders back. Unfortunately, Thighbiter chose that moment to try and bite her on the leg. Again. As she spun in circles, tugging on Thighbiter's reins, Lotta could hear Flay and Flee sniggering.

Scold turned away, bringing her horse into position at the head of the group. Lotta nudged Thighbiter to follow. He did so, barging Flay and her horse out of the way.

'Watch where you're going, snot-face!' Flay snarled, flicking out one of her long silver plaits.

It slapped Lotta in the face. 'Ow!'

Flay smirked and went to pull her plait back – unfortunately that's where it all went wrong. Flay's hair had become tangled around the spikes of Lotta's metal breastplate. She was stuck. Flay gave the plait a hard yank and Lotta lurched sideways half out of her saddle, one foot still caught in Thighbiter's stirrups. The two girls and their horses danced around in tight circles.

'Get HER off me!' Flay shrieked at her sister, who – unhelpfully – grabbed Lotta's arm and tried to pull her away from Flay.

'Get her off ME!' Lotta yelled back. She shook off Flee and started pulling at the hair caught in her armour with one hand while gripping on tightly to Thighbiter's reins with the other. Thighbiter took the opportunity to joyfully try and bite lumps out of everyone.

Scold thundered her way back towards them. 'What's going on here?'

'It's all her fault!'

'She hit me first!'

'Make her let go!'

'She always ruins everything!'

'Neigh!'

Scold snorted, raised an eyebrow, and they all fell silent. Their teacher pulled a short knife out of her belt. 'There seems to be only one thing to do.'

Lotta's eyes grew wide as Scold approached. Flay tried to flinch away but was trapped. In one swift motion Scold leaned forward in her saddle, slicing through the hair caught in Lotta's armour. The girls were free.

Flay slowly straightened up, lifted the remains of her hair in one hand and gazed at it in horror. She now had one long gleaming plait reaching her waist and one silvery tuft that barely reached her shoulder. Her sister's face went completely white.

Lotta slowly pulled the remains of the plait out of her armour. 'Do you want this?' She held out the hair.

Flay snatched at the plait. She closed her eyes and opened her mouth to scream.

'AAAAAAAAAAAAAAAHHHHHHHHHHHHHHHHH!'

It was very loud and very high pitched. The horses all around twitched and flattened their ears.

'We're going to get you for this, Lotta,' Flee hissed as she

31

dragged her shocked sister away. 'Just wait.'

Lotta sighed – nothing new there then. Thighbiter brayed, clearly delighted with himself.

'Flee and Flay, stop sulking – it's only hair,' Scold called to the twins. 'Now, get into line.' Sitting regally astride Thunder Trumper, Scold returned to her position at the head of the group. Flee and Flay grumpily joined them.

'I shall now OPEN THE GATE!' Scold clicked her fingers and Akrid reached for a heavy iron key hanging on the gate post. 'Made by the Dwarves, this key is the only way to open the gates and leave Asgard.' Scold plucked the key out of the girl's fingers. 'NEVER try this without me. You don't want to get lost and end up in the wrong world, do you?'

The Class Two Valkyries giggled as the trainees shook their heads. Although they had all pored over the map of Yggdrasil that hung in Valhalla, picking out the places they had heard of in stories, none of them had ever been allowed to go exploring. Lotta quite fancied a trip to Jotunheim, which was full of snow, or Alfheim, which was made of meadows. But nobody wanted to visit Helheim or Niflheim, the lowest and most miserable of all the Nine Worlds.

'Now,' Scold continued, 'remember to turn your invisibility gauntlets on before we leave.'

'Yeah, we don't want you being spotted and frightening the humans,' called out the girl with deadlocks.

With a wave of relief, Lotta twisted the centre strip of the gauntlet covering her left forearm. Her arm flickered, then vanished, along with the rest of her and Thighbiter. She could do with being invisible for a while, just to stop Flee and Flay giving her the evils. Around her were a series of clicks. Looking towards her fellow trainees, Lotta could hear the sound of gently clinking armour and shifting hooves but could see nothing. With a thump, something struck her helmet, knocking it into her eyes. She thought she heard a muffled snigger.

'Let's do the chant!' Scold bellowed from somewhere in front of her. 'WHO DO WE WANT?'

'Heroes and Great Warriors!'

'WHEN DO WE WANT THEM?'

'Now!'

'WHERE WILL WE PUT THEM?'

'In Valhalla!'

'WHO WILL THEY FIGHT?'

'The Frost Giants!'

'WHEN WILL THEY FIGHT THEM?'

'At Ragnarok!'

'The battle at the end of the world!'

'. . . end of the world!' Lotta echoed. She hoped they had lots of time before then. The Nine Worlds were in balance, at the moment. But you never knew what the Frost Giants were

planning, and when the Giants finally made it into Asgard, Ragnarok would begin. She sighed. It would be embarrassing to still be a Class Three Valkyrie at Ragnarok; you wouldn't get to fight anyone important.

Hooves clopped across the courtyard towards the gateway, and the enormous iron gates swung open. 'TALLY HOoOoOo!' echoed Scold's voice. Sparkling blue hoof prints appeared in the rutted ground, disappearing through the gateway.

Flay and Flee followed swiftly behind with their joint cry of 'For Odin!', their voices coming together to create a weird harmony, which made the hairs on the back of Lotta's neck stand up.

The other Class Three Valkyries galloped along behind them, joining in with their own battle cries.

'Midgard or Bust!'

'Valhalla Forever!'

'Scream If You Want to Go Faster!'

Lotta encouraged a reluctant Thighbiter into a canter. All she had to do now was find a Hero. How hard could that be?

Chapter Three

If They Catch Him,
He'll Be Nailed to the Ceiling

Streaks of a grey dawn appeared over the cliffs in Midgard, but Whetstone was too busy running to appreciate it. Knee-high wet heather ripped holes in his already holey trousers, and the boggy ground sucked unpleasantly at his boots. Behind him he could hear heavy footsteps and bloodthirsty yells.

'COME BACK HERE, YOU DIRTY STINKING WORM!'

Whetstone grinned and sped up. Tucked safely under his cloak was the magical cup he had stolen from the Great Hall.

Now, some magic cups were filled with never-ending mead (a Viking's favourite drink); other cups sang beautiful songs of great Heroes and battles. This cup had a different speciality. In a squeaky metallic and VERY LOUD voice, this cup recited poems like:

> *I once had a good friend named Blot,*
> *Who liked to eat toenails and snot.*
> *It made him feel funny,*
> *So he scratched at his tummy,*
> *And out came an enormous great clot!*

Or:

> *I once drank a cup full of paint,*
> *At first I thought I would faint.*
> *I let out a fart,*
> *Now my pants look like art,*
> *On the whole I think it looks great!*

'Will you shut up?' Whetstone panted. 'You're going to get me caught!'

'Then why don't you take me back?' whined the cup in a voice that sounded like a finger being run around the top of a glass. 'It's not too late.'

Whetstone risked a glance behind him: Awfulrick's Viking horde seemed much closer now. Axes and swords glinted in the weak sunlight. 'Yeah, because Vikings are a really forgiving bunch.'

The cup paused for a moment, then began another poem.

> *There once was a young man who came stealing,*
> *But he had the most peculiar feeling*
> *What he was doing was wrong*
> *When he first heard this song,*
> *If they catch him, he'll be nailed to the ceiling!*

'You are not helping!' Whetstone pulled the cup out from under his cloak. It blinked ruby eyes in the weak sunlight.

Whetstone wrapped his hands around it. 'Listen, you gobby mug. *I* have stolen you, and *I* am going to take you to Cloggibum, where minstrels will make up songs about me and *I'll* be famous. Got it?'

The cup opened its mouth to reply.

'And if you don't stop with those poems,' Whetstone threatened, 'I'm going to take off my slimy socks and stick them in your mouth.'

That seemed to work. The cup fell silent for a moment, but then it started to HUM. Whetstone watched it in disbelief.

'No poems,' the cup explained smugly. 'So no socks.'

'I wouldn't be so sure if I was you.' Whetstone stuffed the cup back under his cloak and tried to ignore the complaints about the smell.

Flat and marshy land stretched all around him, dull in endless shades of brown until it ended suddenly at the cliffs, and the rough grey sea began. Seagulls screamed at him and rabbits skittered away. Up ahead Whetstone could see a small collection of low wooden buildings with heavily thatched roofs. He jogged towards them. Only Vikings would choose somewhere as stupid as this to live. But buildings meant hiding places, and a hiding place was exactly what he needed right now.

A flying axe zipped over the top of his head. Whetstone rolled to the ground, breathless. Seeking shelter behind a large half-buried boulder, the boy came to a stop. His fingers traced the runes carved into the rock.

Ivor the Nose Grinder's farm was small and stuck unhelpfully

against the side of the cliff. Whetstone could hear the waves crashing below. One wrong move and he would be fish food.

Thunder crackled loudly and raindrops began to crash down. Whetstone tried to tuck himself further into the rock for shelter, but it was useless – the rain was coming at him sideways.

A huge hairy man stumbled past, splattering Whetstone with his muddy feet. Whetstone shuddered and pressed himself into his cloak. It was Awfulrick.

'WHERE ARE YOU, YOU LITTLE SLUG?'

Whetstone stuck his finger in his ear to try and block out the noise. The cup twitched in his pocket. 'Remember the socks,' Whetstone hissed, just loud enough for the cup to hear.

Awfulrick stood with his back to Whetstone, the rain turning his bearskin waistcoat into a bath mat. He was so close Whetstone could count the tufty hairs on the back of his neck. The boy held his breath.

'He must have gone the other way, into the caves,' called another voice – Oresmiter the Puffin Eater, Awfulrick's second-in-command. The man in the mangy waistcoat nodded and turned to leave.

Whetstone breathed out slowly. He had done it – he had escaped.

Waiting until Awfulrick's footsteps finished squelching away, the boy dug into the dirt at the base of the boulder with his hands. The near-constant rain had made the ground soft, and before long Whetstone had made a nice deep hole.

'What are you doing?' The cup peeped out of Whetstone's pocket. It sounded worried. 'I don't do mud.'

Whetstone plucked it out from under his cloak and dropped it into the hole. 'You'll be safe here. I'll be back for you soon.'

'NOooo! HELP ME!' The cup started to shriek and jump about, until its tinny voice was drowned by a loud rumble of thunder.

Whetstone filled in the hole and marked the place with a stick of bracken. That would have to do. Now he just needed to find a place to hide until nightfall when he could meet up with Light Finger and Vali at the thieves' camp. Whetstone fixed his eyes on

the buildings that made up Ivor the Nose Grinder's farm —
there was bound to be somewhere there he could hide.

Whetstone slid around the corner of the first building he
came to. A door swung open in the house opposite, making
him flatten himself against the wall. He wasn't keen to run
into Ivor the Nose Grinder. He tried not to look like a
minstrel, just in case. His fingers found a doorframe behind
him, and his nose told him that horses were involved. It must
be a stable.

Holding on tightly to stop the wind crashing it against
the wall, Whetstone edged the door open. It would be warm
(well, warmer) and dry (well, drier) inside, and he didn't think
the horses would mind sharing for one night.

❖

Whetstone settled in to wait for the rain to stop. Ivor the Nose
Grinder's stables were indeed dry and warm, if a bit horsey.
More importantly though, no one would come to bother him.
He stretched out on some empty straw and tried to ignore the
sound of the wind, which was attempting to rip the roof off.

He laced his fingers behind his head and allowed himself
a smug smile. Not bad for his first theft. Good thing Viking
Heroes are known more for the size of their muscles than their
brains. Whetstone had heard that Awfulrick won his magic
cup by fighting a Giant. But to do that, he would have had to
cross from the human world of Midgard into the land of the
Giants, and no one had ever done that.

Back in Drott, the Angry Bogey had liked to tell stories about the other worlds, especially the land of the Giants. Her stories used to give Whetstone nightmares, full of bloodthirsty monsters and endless winter. Her descriptions were so realistic, it was as if she believed she had been there. But that was impossible. Although, she also believed that the orphaned wolves were her babies and that chickens could read minds.

There had been a time when Whetstone would lie awake at night, waiting for someone, anyone, to come and take him away from the Angry Bogey. He used to dream that he had been lost, not abandoned, and that someone out there was searching for him. Travellers from a far-off land, maybe. But no one ever came, and eventually Whetstone stopped dreaming.

But now he had a new dream. Light Finger was going to be so impressed when he made it back to the camp.

Stories of his adventures might even make it back to Drott. He imagined visiting there after news of his epic deeds had spread. People would be chanting his name, throwing flowers. He would be popular, and no one would make jokes about him smelling of dog breath or not having any parents ever again. Thieving might not be the Viking way, but everyone appreciated a good story. His days of having to clean out the wolf kennels were OVER.

The stable door rattled on its hinges. The boy turned and leaned up on one elbow. 'Vali, is that you?'

No answer – just the wind. The last person Whetstone wanted to see was Vali. He was always sneaking around, and Whetstone was sure he would try to get the cup for himself.

Whetstone rolled over and snuggled into his cloak, wondering what Vali's problem was. It wasn't Whetstone's fault Vali messed up his chance to get the cup – that happened before Whetstone had joined up with him and Light Finger. For the hundredth time, Whetstone tried to figure out why Light Finger was so keen to get his hands on the cup. He had told Whetstone the cup knew things, but the only thing Whetstone could see it knowing was how to be annoying.

THUMP.

Whetstone sat up, his senses on red alert. One of the horses whinnied in their stall. Someone was here. Someone who shouldn't be here. Well, someone *else* who shouldn't be here. Whetstone shifted cautiously, trying not to make any noise. Shuffling forward, he carefully peeked out into the wider stables.

THUMP.

A blinding pain in his head sent him tumbling to the floor. His head throbbed and his vision blurred. He blinked – the stables were now sideways.

With a dull thud, a length of wood dropped on to the ground next to him. Whetstone was dimly aware of fingers rummaging through his pockets. 'Gerroff,' he muttered, trying to lift his head.

The fingers stopped. Whetstone sensed movement behind him – someone was searching through the straw. Footsteps approached as Whetstone fought to keep his eyes open. Pale hands grabbed the front of his tunic and pulled him into a sitting position.

'Where is it? Where's the cup?'

'Vali?' Whetstone asked dumbly. 'Wha—'

The hands released him, and Whetstone slumped back on to the floor. Outside, the storm howled and the footsteps retreated.

Straw was heaped on top of him.

'Gerroff . . . 's tickly,' Whetstone slurred. The warmth made his eyes close; blackness washed over him. Maybe it would all make sense in the morning.

Chapter Four

A Lotta Mistakes

Lotta's first journey into the world of Midgard had started out well enough. Following the sound of Scold's battle cries, the trainees on their flying warhorses soared out through the gates of Asgard, just like proper Valkyries.

They looped around the top of Yggdrasil's trunk, enormous leaves fluttering in the breeze as they descended. Lotta spotted signposts hanging in the branches: one showed the way to the temples of Vanaheim, and below that another sign pointed towards the Elves in Alfheim. Under a domed sky Midgard lay directly beneath them, perched between the trunk and a sturdy branch.

It was beautiful, if you didn't mind heights.

A few hours later they crossed into Midgard, a storm began, and everything went wrong. It turns out that despite Thighbiter's tough attitude, in reality the horse had a serious problem with thunder.

They dropped further
and further behind the others,
but Lotta didn't dare call out. Valkyries were supposed to be excellent horse riders. It was one of the things they were tested on, and Lotta was already on her last warning. She couldn't give Scold any more reasons to fail her. If Lotta couldn't be a Valkyrie, she didn't know what she would do.

Lotta had been born in a battle to the far south of Krud, in a land where tall palm trees cast shade on to the dusty desert, and stone buildings with curved arches nestled against rocky outcrops. She may not be naturally talented at transformation, or horse riding, or . . . fighting, but she *was* a Valkyrie and she was determined to show everyone she could do anything the others could. Even if that meant riding her bad-tempered horse through a storm.

Grey, choppy water surged under Thighbiter's hooves. Lotta bent low over the horse's neck. 'Come on, Thighbiter – just a bit further. If we don't keep up, they'll get to the battle and head back to Asgard without us.' Lotta wasn't sure how long collecting fallen warriors would take, but she doubted Scold would want to hang about.

Thighbiter snorted in agreement, but seconds later a *CRASH* and a blinding flash of light made the horse panic and lunge for the ground.

Thighbiter landed with a *splash, spliSH, GURGLE, squish.* Lotta clutched the horse's neck to stop herself from falling. The invisibility gauntlet on her wrist clicked in a broken-sounding way, and both she and Thighbiter popped back into sight.

'Trust me to get a dodgy one.' Lotta sat up, twisting the central band and trying to get it to work. She and the warhorse flickered but stayed resolutely visible.

Pushing her helmet up from over her eyes, Lotta looked around. They had landed in a damp brown scrubby patch of land next to the cliffs. Big rocks and brambles were dotted all around. No arrows, swords, enormous hairy men or hungry ravens, though. In fact, there was no sign of a battle anywhere. Lotta's heart sank. 'We must be miles off course.' She wiped rain off her face.

The sea pounded against rocks somewhere in the murk, and in the distance sat a group of squat Viking buildings. A large boulder stood alone in the middle of the field. Thighbiter squelched towards it. Lotta read:

> *Ivor the Nose Grinder*
> *Gerroff my land!*
> *Travelling minstrels will*
> *be force-fed cabbage*
> *till they burst!*

'Good thing I'm not musical.'

Thighbiter tossed his mane in agreement, intentionally showering her with raindrops. Lotta grimaced, feeling the water seep through her black curls and drip down her neck. She slid down from the saddle, landing with a squelch. Hooking Thighbiter's reins over his head, she led him towards the nearest building. With any luck someone there would be able to tell her where the nearest battle was and they could get back on track.

Lotta slowed down as they approached the farm. She glanced uneasily at Thighbiter's head and body armour. It had been made by the finest Dwarf craftsmen out of leather and iron. It was beautiful, elaborate and very scary to look at, covered in spikes and pictures of snarling faces. In Asgard it looked magnificent, but down here in the human world it looked a bit . . . out of place. Lotta rubbed her neck. Maybe walking into a Viking home with a heavily armoured horse wasn't such a good idea – people would be bound to ask questions.

Lotta loitered behind one of the buildings, debating

whether to leave Thighbiter somewhere and go in by herself. If she took off her helmet, she might pass for a Viking, or a lost traveller, someone human at least. She absolutely *had* to find out where Scold and the others were. A whinny came from a nearby building. Lotta peeked inside and found a stable. Perfect.

❈

It took a moment for Lotta's eyes to adjust to the darkness. It was good to be out of the rain, and now that all four hooves were back on the ground, Thighbiter seemed to be recovering his old bad attitude. He leered at a squat pony who was chewing hay nearby.

Lotta spotted an empty stall at the end of the row and led Thighbiter towards it. Her Valkyrie shield glowed faintly, giving them just enough light to see by. The other horses whinnied and snickered at their strange appearance.

'*Excuse me*,' she muttered to herself. '*You don't happen to know if there's a battle anywhere around here, do you?* No, I can't say that.'

Thighbiter gave a snort, which sounded exactly like a laugh.

She stepped into the empty stall. 'Be quiet – this is all your fault.' The straw looked thick and lumpy. Her foot brushed against something. *Funny*, she thought, poking at the straw with her boot. *That almost looks like . . . a leg.*

Lotta stopped. She knelt down and brushed the straw away. It *was* a leg. And a foot . . . and a body. Lotta pushed more straw away, following an arm up to a shoulder, then to a head. It belonged to a boy with dirty blond hair and ragged clothing. Lotta's nose wrinkled. *When did he last have a wash? And what in all of Midgard is he doing asleep buried in straw?*

Lotta poked him with the metal toecap of her boot. 'Oi, are you OK?'

The boy didn't answer.

Rummaging in the straw, Lotta found one of the boy's hands and lifted it. It felt cold and clammy and had very grubby fingernails. Lotta let go and his arm dropped heavily back down with a *SMACK*. The boy's head lolled to one side and his eyes remained closed.

A prickle ran up Lotta's spine. She stumbled out of the stall, bumping into Thighbiter, who snorted at her as she pulled him towards the open door. 'I think we should get out of here,' she muttered.

In the doorway, Thighbiter twitched his ears and gave a whinny of recognition. Lotta tipped her head backwards to gaze up at the sky. Flickering on the edge of her vision was a collection of riders on flying horses. The pounding of their hooves blending in with the thunder. Lotta could just make out the mighty horns of Scold's helmet, followed by a flash of silver, which she was sure was one of the twin's hair.

Lotta's heart dropped. 'They're on their way back to Asgard. I can't believe I missed my first battle.' She slumped against the doorway, accidentally getting one of the spikes on her helmet stuck in the splintery wood. 'Once Scold realizes we're not there and haven't brought back a fallen warrior, that'll be it. I'll be stuck as a Class Three Valkyrie forever.'

Thighbiter pawed at the ground, keen to join the others.

'Oh, so *now* you fancy a bit of flying, do you?' Lotta grumbled, trying to pull her helmet free. Thighbiter looked a bit ashamed.

Lotta gave up on her helmet and leaned back against the horse's warm body. 'It's no use. Even if we could catch up, we don't have anyone to bring back . . . from . . . the battle . . .'

In unison, the horse and wannabe Valkyrie turned their heads to look back into the straw-filled darkness behind them.

❋

Ten minutes later, horse and rider were pounding through the sky, faster than they'd ever flown, and catching up with the crowd of Valkyries ahead. Thighbiter's legs pumped and thrashed, charging out through the edge of Midgard's domed sky and following Yggdrasil's trunk upward past the branches that led to the other worlds.

Lotta bent low over the horse's neck, urging him onward. In front of her, resting awkwardly across the saddle, was the unmoving form of the boy. Lotta crossed her fingers, hoping that whatever had happened to him had been Heroic.

Asgard appeared ahead of them, rising like an island out of the topmost branches of the world tree. A bronze sky hung above the city, and tall white walls stretched as far as the eye could see, towering out of lush grass. A warning was chiselled into the enormous walls. It read:

FROST GIANTS KEEP OUT

Beneath it and in different handwriting, someone else had carved:

Loki smels of poOo

Just outside the walls the air shimmered as Scold popped back into full vision, her horse prancing on the grass. With a series of clicks, the rest of the trainees reappeared. They clustered around Scold, horses snorting and steaming. Lotta and Thighbiter snuck into position at the back and tried to look as if they had been there all along. A bead of sweat trickled behind Lotta's ear as she tried to control her breathing.

After a quick squint at the trainees, Scold reached into her pocket and produced the heavy key to unlock the gates.

51

Flay scowled at Lotta from beneath her helmet. She went to toss a plait over her shoulder, but her fingers closed around a short tuft instead. Her mouth curled into a snarl.

Flee noticed and glanced behind her at the boy lying across Lotta's saddle. She nudged her sister. 'Look at the state of him – he's not even wearing any armour,' she said with a snigger.

Lotta's brown skin felt hot and prickly; she flicked the corner of the boy's cloak over his face.

'Very well done, ladies,' called Scold. 'All that is left to do is to deliver your Heroes and warriors to the hall of Valhalla.' She gestured at the massive wooden building looming through the gates.

The trainee Valkyries formed into a line, Lotta and Thighbiter lingering at the back. Lotta's heart thudded painfully. All she had to do was get the boy past Scold and they would be safe.

She watched Flay trot confidently towards the gates, a warrior slumped easily over her saddle. He was enormous, with a scratchy red beard and blue battle tattoos. Scold gave a nod and Flay smiled. Next came Flee, her warrior almost as large and hairy. She was followed by the other trainees. A small girl struggled to keep her warrior on her horse – he kept slipping to one side, forcing her to hold on tightly to the back of his tunic.

Then it was Lotta's turn. Pushing her shoulders back and her chin up, she urged Thighbiter into a careful trot.

'Wait!'

Lotta's heart sped up into a whirr. Scold approached,

looking curiously at the bundle lying over Thighbiter's saddle. Reaching out one tanned hand, she twitched the cloak aside, revealing the boy's face.

'He's a bit young, isn't he?'

Lotta clamped her lips together and smiled. She didn't trust herself to speak. A second bead of sweat crept out from under her helmet.

Scold peered closely at the boy. Then, to Lotta's amazement, she nodded, and Thighbiter trotted onward. Lotta breathed out and her fingers – which had been gripping the reins so tightly her knuckles cracked – relaxed.

Unfortunately, just when everything seemed to be going right, the bundle on Lotta's saddle gave a great snore. '*NWAA-ARR!*'

Lotta jumped in shock; even Thighbiter wobbled a bit.

Scold's head shot round. 'What was that?'

'*GWARGH, HARK, hack, hack.*' Lotta faked a coughing fit. She clutched her chest in explanation. The boy twitched against her leg, and Lotta urged Thighbiter into a faster trot. Under Scold's beady eyes they passed through the great gates and into Asgard.

Lotta thought she might pass out with terror. If Scold found out she had brought a living human into the world of the Gods, she would be in the worst trouble *ever*. Her mess-up in Valhalla with the *Saga of Svenson the Selfish* would be nothing compared to this. She had been so *sure* he was dead. He was cold, he was still. He was . . . waking up!

Her hands slipped on the reins as she looked around in panic, but nobody paid any attention. The real fallen warriors were beginning to change. Their bodies gaining the magical blue glow that marked them out as the guests of Odin. Lotta's thoughts spun. She couldn't take him to Valhalla – it was obvious that he was still alive. She needed a hiding place . . . and quick.

Chapter Five

Pink, Cuddly Dragons

Whetstone groaned. It felt like someone was tap dancing inside his head in metal boots. Memories started catching up with him.

> *Asgard, Asgard,*
> *Home of Gods and stealing,*
> *Don't let them catch you or*
> *You'll be nailed to the ceiling?*

Then lots of shouting, people chasing him . . . But he had got away and buried the stolen cup, hadn't he? And then he'd found that stable.

Rough breathing came from somewhere nearby. That meant people and, judging by the sound of the breathing, it was big people. Whetstone kept his eyes closed. He wasn't sure where he was, and once people realized he was awake, things might start happening. Things he wasn't ready for.

Slowly he stretched out his fingers, but instead of the straw he was expecting, he found cloth and furs. That meant . . .

a bed? The last time he had slept in anything close to a bed was at the Angry Bogey's rescue home, but it is hard for a boy to sleep comfortably in a dog basket.

A smell reached his nostrils – it wasn't bad exactly, but sort of warm . . .

Sour . . .

Sharp . . .

And a bit like dog biscuits. Whetstone turned his head and peeled one eye open. He found himself staring at the longest teeth, in the biggest mouth he had ever seen.

'*ARRRRGGGGGHHHH!*' With a jump, Whetstone pushed himself up and away from the enormous jaws. Stars flashed before his eyes and the pain in his head made him feel sick.

A huge grey dog sat watching him – so big, Whetstone thought it must be a wolf. His stomach twisted into knots, afraid that it had all been a dream, and that he was back with the Angry Bogey.

He stared frantically around, expecting to see the inside of her kennels, but instead found he was inside a smallish wooden room. Furs, brightly patterned blankets and carved furniture danced in front of his panicked eyes.

The dog, wolf – whatever it was – hadn't moved. It sat at the side of the bed and watched him with mismatched eyes – one blue, one brown. A long line of drool hung from its jagged teeth.

'Good doggy.' Whetstone tried to shuffle down the bed away from the beast. The dog shifted to follow him. Whetstone froze. A scar on his arm twinged unpleasantly, a souvenir from one of the Angry Bogey's *furry babies*, a Snapping Shadow Wolf who had decided that a toddler-sized Whetstone looked like lunch. Whetstone rubbed his arm slowly, trying not to look at the wolf-dog's long curved teeth.

Except . . . wolves weren't usually found inside, and not even the Angry Bogey was mad enough to put collars on them. Not even collars with big metal spikes like this one.

'Nice doggy,' he said. 'Good doggy, please don't eat me.' The dog opened its mouth and a long pink tongue lolled out. Whetstone wasn't sure if this was an improvement.

He hesitated, then slowly stretched out a hand. But the dog didn't snap at him, so Whetstone reached over and rubbed it carefully behind the ears. The dog closed its funny mismatched eyes and panted.

He eyed the dog's collar, which had a name tag in the shape of an axe hanging from it.

'*Broken Tooth.*'

The dog opened its eyes at the sound of its name.

Whetstone sat back. His head throbbed. Reaching up, he found an egg-sized lump sticking up under his hair. He winced as his fingers prodded it, wondering if he should invest in one of those metal helmets after all.

The boy looked around, puzzled. The last thing he could remember was the stable in which he had been hiding from Chief Awfulrick and his horde of hooligans. But this definitely wasn't a stable, and he couldn't imagine Awfulrick giving him a bed if he caught him. More likely he would give Whetstone a shove off the nearest cliff.

There was a distinctly bedroomy feel to the place. In fact, quite a girly bedroomy feel. On the wall opposite was a large poster, some drippy-looking boys pouting out at the room. *The Vanir*, Whetstone read. And below in more swirly writing: *Frey, Heimdall and Njord*. Frey had a ridiculous haircut, and Njord was wearing stupid trousers.

Whetstone cast his eyes over the room. Clothing was scattered untidily across a diamond-patterned rug, and in a brightly woven bowl lay a hairbrush with several long black hairs trapped in it.

Putting his hand back to steady himself, Whetstone found he was squashing a whole family of cuddly dragons in a range of colours and sizes, which had been tucked in next to the pillow. He pulled his hand back quickly and Broken Tooth licked him. Whetstone wiped the dribble off his face with the pinkest of the dragons.

Somehow he had ended up in a girl's bedroom. He had to get out of here and back to Light Finger before she, whoever she was, came back. Whetstone slid his legs off the bed and on to the rug. His head spun as he tried standing up, and he gulped down the swirling nausea.

Using Broken Tooth for support, he crept towards the door. He could sense movement outside and the sound of distant voices. The door was not locked. Whetstone pulled it open a crack and looked out into the world beyond. His mouth dropped open.

Broken Tooth bumped into his legs, knocking him through the doorway and out into a wide rutted street. He was in a sort of village, but one unlike any he had visited before. Not even Bore, which was buried deep in the caves outside Spindle Mountains, or Dulge, which floated on the marshes to the far west.

Broken Tooth followed him out and sat on his haunches, panting. The door banged shut behind them, but Whetstone ignored it; he was too busy gawping.

The THIRD thing Whetstone noticed was the sky. It wasn't blue or grey like he was used to, but bronze.

The SECOND thing he noticed was the buildings. They were wooden with thatched roofs and decorative carvings, just like normal Viking homes, but these were HUGE. Easily four or five times as big as the biggest house he had ever seen. Each one looked like the hall of a Great Chief.

But the FIRST thing he noticed was the people. There were dozens of Vikings here – and they were all GLOWING!

A tall, tanned woman strode past him carrying an axe. A bright yellow glow surrounded her, reminding Whetstone of the sun shining out from behind a cloud. But the glow wasn't coming from behind her; it was coming from inside her, out of her hair and skin. With barely a glance, she swept past Whetstone, continuing down the path.

Whetstone jumped back as an older, dark-skinned girl in armour marched past him in the opposite direction. He stumbled, trying not to land on Broken Tooth, who licked him. The girl tossed back her long dreadlocks and threw out her arms. With a loud *CRACK* the girl vanished, and a large bird appeared in mid-air. It squawked at Whetstone before swooping away.

'Oh, this isn't good,' Whetstone muttered, closing his eyes and leaning back against the door. 'Now I'm seeing things.'

Broken Tooth whined in sympathy and stuck his wet nose against Whetstone's arm. Whetstone opened his eyes again, expecting the world to tilt and spin around him. But it didn't.

Up ahead, he could see an open area, a bit like a market square. Colours flashed as people moved about, filling the space with light. Drums and rattles boomed for a moment, fighting with the sound of chatter and merchants selling their wares. The scent of strange spices drifted in the air.

'C'mon,' Whetstone muttered to Broken Tooth, pulling up his hood. 'I need to find a healer – that bump on my head must be making me hallucinate. The cup will be safe at Ivor the Nose Grinder's farm until I figure out where I am.'

Every house he passed seemed to be larger and more magnificent than the one before. Some had two, three or even four floors (which may not sound like much to you, but it's a lot when all you have to build with is wood and mud).

'Light Finger said he was going to take me to the city of Cloggibum – maybe this is it?' Whetstone muttered as he stopped to gaze at a house with fruit carved around the door posts. 'But that doesn't explain why I ended up in a girl's bedroom. And I never thought Cloggibum would look like THIS.' He stuffed his hands in his pockets. 'Ha, Light Finger is going to be so annoyed when he finds out I left the cup back in Krud.'

The houses were painted in bright colours, some green, others blue or purple. Each house had a huge set of doors with a symbol set into them in shining metal. They passed a sword, a bear, a boar, and on a particularly dramatic set of red doors, a large cat.

Whetstone tried not to stare – no one else appeared to find

it unusual at all. 'Wow. If being a thief means I get to live like this, I would've done it sooner.'

He paused to look at a low, dark house. A pair of silver snakes glittered on the door, their eyes picked out in bright jewels. Whetstone took a step towards them; Broken Tooth growled and nudged him with his wet nose. 'All right – I'm just looking.'

Whetstone soon forgot all about the snakes when ahead of him he saw the largest and most amazing building yet. Easily the size of the whole of Krud, the walls were made of row upon row of painted shields, and when he tipped his head back, Whetstone could just make out that instead of straw or reeds, the roof was made of thousands of spears.

The delicious smell of roasting meat wafted out from the half-open doors. Whetstone's tummy rumbled. The last food he'd eaten had been Ethel's horrible stew – and you could hardly call that food.

Broken Tooth licked the drool from his lips.

'Hungry, boy?'

The wolf looked up at him with big eyes.

'Me too.'

Whetstone followed the smell towards the doors. Picked out in silver swirls was a pair of large birds with bright eyes that flashed and quivered in the light.

'I guess they're supposed to be Odin's ravens.' Whetstone reached out to touch them. 'The people in this place are REALLY into religion.' He stopped, his fingers inches away from the carved metal.

'That's it! That's what's so strange! There's a house for each God or Goddess. Look.' He pointed towards the symbol on a large, squat building. 'A hammer for Thor, God of Thunder.' Gesturing towards the red doors. 'A cat for the Goddess of Love, Freyja. And there, snakes for Loki, the Trickster.' He faced the ravens again. 'And these are for Odin, Chief of the Gods.'

Broken Tooth licked his hand encouragingly.

'Maybe this isn't a real village at all?' Whetstone puzzled, stepping away from the doors and following the side of the building down a nearby street. 'Maybe it's a sort of amusement park where people go to celebrate the Gods, like . . . Asgard-land? Where you can dress up as your favourite God or Goddess, look round their pretend Great Hall, maybe even go on Valkyrie rides and buy a souvenir shield?' Whetstone ran his hand along a fence post covered in carved bees. 'It feels real enough – you could almost believe you were in Asgard. I wonder if there's some kind of show where the Frost Giants attack and the Gods have to fight them off?'

Broken Tooth whimpered. Whetstone scratched his ears absent-mindedly. 'I bet people pay a lot of money to come here. Bring the kids, you know – a fun day out for all the family.'

Behind them a door slammed open. The dog sniffed the air and whined, his ears lying flat against his head.

Whetstone twisted the edge of his cloak between his fingers. 'But what am I doing here? I don't think Light Finger is into fun days out.'

63

'Where's that blasted dog?' bellowed a female voice, making Whetstone jump. A woman appeared on the steps of the raven building. She peered about, her hands on her hips. 'Broken Tooth, I know you're here somewhere – there's dog hair in Valhalla again!'

Broken Tooth whined and cowered, trying to hide behind Whetstone's legs.

'Sorry, Scold. I'll go and look for him,' called a girl's voice.

At the sound of her voice, Broken Tooth lunged forward, knocking the boy against the fence. Whetstone flung his arm out to break his fall. A panel shifted under him, the boy and dog tumbling through. They landed in a sunny flower bed on the other side. The fence panel shifted back into position with a creak.

Whetstone glanced around. They were outside the low dark house he had spotted earlier. Carved snakes twisted along the house's wooden beams; they seemed to move by themselves. Whetstone rubbed his eyes, blaming a trick of the light.

A window stood open. Disentangling himself from the dog, Whetstone crept forward. Hearing a voice from inside, he instinctively ducked down, hiding below the painted shutters.

'I can't believe you came back empty-handed, after all the fuss you made,' said a woman's voice. 'You said it was important.'

'I couldn't get it,' replied a sulky voice Whetstone thought he recognized. 'You brought me back too soon.'

'You're pathetic!' raged a man. 'I knew I shouldn't have trusted you.'

Whetstone shuffled around to peek in through a crack in the shutters. He could see a sliver of a luxuriously decorated room with lush red-and-gold tapestries hanging from the walls. A glowing woman with elaborate plaits stood with her back to him. Beyond her, a tall, pale man in a red tunic paced up and down. He kept appearing and disappearing as he walked past the woman. Their faces turned towards something Whetstone could not see.

'I was so close,' the man fumed. Whetstone flinched at the crash of something being kicked over. 'Twelve years I've been working on this plan, but this numbskull had to mess it all up.'

A flash of green light came from inside the room. Whetstone ran his hand over his face, trying to clear his vision.

'Stop it!' the woman cried. 'You'll hurt him!'

'Good! Then maybe he'll learn something.'

Whetstone peeked through the window again and saw a familiar ghostly-white figure with dark-rimmed eyes sliding into a chair.

'I told you, it wasn't my fault.' Vali ran his hand through his hair. A flickering orange glow surrounded him. 'I left him asleep in the stable while I looked for the cup.'

Whetstone swallowed, his mouth dry, the realization that they were talking about him sinking in.

Footsteps halted as the man stopped pacing and contemplated Vali with a sneer. 'You couldn't find a pebble on a beach. You know how important this is. I had the boy, and I nearly had the cup too. The plan can't progress without them.'

Whetstone's eyebrows shot up into his hairline as he tried to figure out what plan they were talking about. The only plan he knew of was Light Finger's one to get the cup and make him famous, although it seemed as if Vali wasn't really working for Light Finger after all. He wanted to get the cup for these people instead.

'Now the boy and the cup are missing. How convenient,' the man said in a low voice.

'What's that supposed to mean?' Vali snapped back. The chair scraped against the floor as he rose to his feet.

'That cup has many powers,' the man continued softly. 'Maybe SOMEONE isn't sticking to the plan, Vali.'

'I did – you know I did!'

'I've spent *years* trying to get my hands on that tatty mug. Years of sucking up to Odin and Frigg, playing the fool. Waiting for the boy to get old enough to be of any use. Waiting for my moment to come. The boy was my best shot at seizing power, and *you lost him*?!'

Whetstone's mind spun, trying to take in everything they were saying. If Vali didn't know where Whetstone was, maybe it hadn't been Light Finger who took him out of Krud after all.

'Do you think the boy ran off with it?' The woman moved to stand next to Vali; she put her hand on his shoulder. 'Maybe he knows more than you think. He was brought up by that . . . woman, after all.'

The man leaned against the table. The movement threw strange shadows against the wall. This one looked like a bear, no . . . a fox, or maybe a snake. 'He has no idea what it is, or who he is. He's harmless.'

Whetstone bristled.

The woman spoke again. 'Well, I'm not sorry that he's gone. I always thought it was cruel of you to involve him.'

'HE *IS* INVOLVED!' the man shouted, slamming his hand down on the table. The others shushed him. Whetstone ducked down lower.

'He has *always* been involved,' the man repeated more quietly. 'Why else do you think he ended up in Drott under her care?'

Whetstone's breath caught in his chest. How did they know so much about him?

Vali sniggered. 'You always said you were so great and powerful, but now you need help from a worm.' A thud and an 'Ow!' followed, as though someone had just clipped him around the ear.

'Don't speak to your father like that!' the woman snapped, followed by another flash of green light and a yell.

Whetstone dropped on to his hands and knees, keen to get away from Vali's parents. He had thought the Angry Bogey was bad. No wonder Vali was desperate to get his hands on the cup.

'Stop doing that!' Vali cried.

'Then start paying attention,' the man barked. 'We need the boy because: One – he's the only one who knows where the cup is now . . .' Another flash and a bang. 'Two – you know what will happen if *I* touch it, idiot.'

'That's not *my* fault. You shouldn't have had that argument with Frigg and Odin.'

'And three – we need the boy to ask the cup for the riddle. He's the only one who can do it. I can't finish the Skera Harp without him.'

Feeling sorry for Vali for having to deal with his parents, Whetstone crawled sideways away from the window. Not sorry enough to give him the cup though.

SNAP!

Whetstone froze as his knee landed on a twig. The voices inside the house stopped abruptly and quick footsteps approached the window. Whetstone dived behind a nearby bush, trying not to breathe too loudly.

The woman called out brightly, 'Who's there?'

Whetstone's heart hammered wildly in his chest. He looked around for the dog. Broken Tooth was sitting right in front of the window; there was no way they could miss him.

'Broken Tooth!' Whetstone beckoned to the dog. But the dog was more interested in trying to catch a flea, a ferocious expression on his face as he nibbled at his own leg.

The window shutters opened, and Vali appeared, the orange glow surrounding him and the dark shadows under his eyes giving his face a fox-like expression. Whetstone's stomach rumbled loudly as the sweet smell of apples cooking rolled out of the window.

'It's that wolf.' Vali leaned through the window. 'The dopey-looking one.' Broken Tooth looked up, a hurt expression on his fuzzy face. 'How did he get in here?'

The shutters were pushed further open, and Vali's mother peered out into the garden. 'He'd better not be pooing.

It will destroy my begonias!'

'Get rid of him,' Vali's father called from inside the house.

Vali waved his arm out of the window at Broken Tooth. 'Go on – scat!'

Broken Tooth sniffed. Then, following the scent of food, he lolloped over towards the window, his tongue hanging out.

'I said, *go*!' Vali picked up a painted stone sitting on the windowsill and chucked it in Broken Tooth's direction. It bounced off the ground and hit the dog on the nose. Broken Tooth cried out and Whetstone's eyes watered in sympathy. The dog turned and bounded away, jumping the wooden fence back on to the busy street. A high-pitched shriek came from beyond the fence as a wolf unexpectedly landed on someone's head. Vali laughed mirthlessly and returned to the house, pulling the shutters closed behind him.

Whetstone stood up carefully, picking his way out from behind the bush. He crept towards a wicker gate that led out of the garden. Voices drifted after him.

'I'll have to go back,' Vali's father said from inside the house. 'Find the boy before it's too late.'

'I'll go,' Vali offered. 'I'll get him, and the cup too.'

'You?' The man laughed. 'If I wanted another complete failure, I'd ask you. No, I have a better idea. They say Valkyries are good at picking the right person out of a crowd.'

'The Valkyries work for Odin – they won't help you.'

'We'll see about that. There's always someone who's keen for a favour.'

Chapter Six

Goddess of Pushing
People Over

Whetstone stumbled out of the gate and back on to the main road. Hoping to put Vali and his weird family behind him, he took a few random turns leading down narrow twisting lanes. His mind was full of the conversation he had just overheard. Vali's father wanted the cup. Whetstone bristled. He hadn't gone to all the effort of stealing it just to have someone else take it. What about his Fortune and Glory? And what was all that rubbish about Whetstone knowing a riddle? He shook his head. He resolved to find Light Finger and get out of here – wherever *here* was – quickly.

The dull clunk and clatter of a loom being used came from somewhere nearby. Whetstone followed the sound around the corner and found a low open window. Sitting innocently on the window ledge was a delicious-looking loaf of bread. His mouth watered. Bread was normal, familiar. Bread would stop the churning in his stomach and make everything all right. He glanced over his shoulder – the street was empty. He reached out a hand . . .

'HEY!'

Something whacked into Whetstone from behind, knocking him face first into the hard ground. Something with four massive paws and smelly breath.

'Broken Tooth!' he gasped, trying to push the wolf off and sit up. Hands reached down and pulled the dog away by its collar. Whetstone shoved his cloak out of his face to see a girl with brown skin and black hair wearing a *very* cross expression.

'Who are you?' He thought of the black hair left in the hairbrush and the pink cuddly dragon now covered in dog dribble. 'Is Broken Tooth yours?'

'Yes, now shhhh!' The girl pulled him to his feet.

Whetstone found himself abruptly wrapped in thick fabric, a metal helmet hastily shoved on top. The lump on his head throbbed, making lights flash in front of his eyes. 'What are you doing?' he spluttered, trying to make a hole in the cloth to breathe through.

'Getting you out of here . . . There was a mistake. You have to go.' She grabbed his arm and propelled him away through the twisting lanes.

Whetstone tried to stop, but the girl was surprisingly strong for her size. He twisted around to duck out of the blanket she had thrown over him but ended up getting more tangled. Whetstone wobbled, felt himself overbalance, and landed heavily on his knees. The helmet fell to the floor with a clang. Broken Tooth started licking all the bits of him he could reach. The girl sighed and tried to pull Whetstone back up on his feet.

'What's going on?' Whetstone sat stubbornly on the ground. 'I'm not going anywhere till I get some answers.'

The girl stood over him, hands on hips. She looked like she wanted to kick him. Whetstone glared at her to show he meant business. The girl glared back, her black eyebrows knitting together like angry caterpillars. Eventually she sighed, her shoulders slumping. She tucked a stray curl behind her ear.

'It's a long story. Don't freak out but – you're in Asgard.'

Whetstone raised his eyebrows. 'Yeah, right – I might have banged my head, but I'm not stupid.'

'Idiot humans.' The girl rolled her eyes. 'Look around you – this is Asgard. You know, the place where the Gods live?'

'And who are you?' Whetstone asked, shrugging out of the blanket. 'Brunhilda – Goddess of Pushing People Over?'

The girl gritted her teeth.

'I guess that makes me Whetstone – God of Thieves.' He snickered.

'Whetstone?' The girl snorted. 'What sort of stupid name is that?'

'Shut up.' Whetstone crossed his arms. 'You're just annoyed I'm not falling for your silly "This is Asgard" game.'

The girl gawked at him. 'I'm not playing a game,' she said at last. 'And my name isn't Brunhilda. It's Lotta. But I did quite enjoy pushing you over.'

'Ha!'

'Wait – you really ARE in Asgard, and I can prove it.'

Whetstone ignored her. 'Whatever.' He shoved Broken Tooth away and got to his feet. He had to get the cup to Light Finger at the thieves' camp before Vali, or his dad, found it. Dumping the blanket and helmet in her arms, Whetstone walked away from the girl. He heard her mutter something under her breath, but then her metal studded boots thudded after him. Ducking through an archway, he spotted a long wooden building: a stable. Maybe he could, ahem, *borrow* a horse to help him on his way back to Krud. He could ask for directions when he was away from this odd 'Lotta' girl.

Whetstone entered the building. Horses of all colours and sizes pawed at the ground. A glimmer of gold caught his eye. In the last stall stood a magnificent horse with bright eyes, a shining golden coat and . . . EIGHT LEGS. Whetstone blinked, but none of the legs vanished. Four at the front and four at the back. He slowed to a stop, staring at the impossible horse.

Lotta caught up with him. 'That's Sleipnir –' she reached out to stroke the horse's nose – 'Odin's horse. You know: one eye, big beard, likes ravens.'

'But that's . . . That's . . .'

'Asgard,' Lotta explained. 'I did try to tell you.' She set her mouth in a determined line. 'But you have to go, or we'll both be in big trouble.' She dumped the helmet back on his head and began to shove Whetstone away from the golden horse. 'We're just lucky no one has noticed you're not glowing yet.'

Whetstone stumbled on the rutted ground. 'Wait a minute – I don't understand. *Gods* live in Asgard, not people like me. Unless . . .' He turned to face Lotta. 'I'm not dead, am I?'

'I wish.'

'Thanks.'

Lotta cleared her throat, awkwardly. 'There was a bit of a mix-up,' she admitted. 'I thought you WERE dead. I'm a Valkyrie.'

Whetstone nearly fell over again. 'A WHAT!?!'

Sleipnir whinnied. The girl glanced around. 'Be quiet or we're going to get caught.'

'But you're a . . . a . . .'

'A Valkyrie! Don't tell me you don't know what a Valkyrie is?'

Whetstone goggled at her.

Lotta sighed. 'Shield maiden of Odin, Bringer of the Dead . . . Wait – you do know who Odin is, right?'

Whetstone felt his mouth drop open – he could only nod.

'I wouldn't ask, but you seem particularly thick, even for a human.'

Whetstone closed his mouth with a click.

In a sing-song voice, Lotta continued. 'Valkyries swoop low over battlefields collecting the best warriors to build Odin's army. They're going to help us fight the Frost Giants at Ragnarok. Until then, they wait in his great hall – Valhalla.' She pointed at the roof of spears that poked up over the other buildings. 'You might have heard of it?'

Whetstone peered dumbly at the building. 'That's Valhalla?'

'Yes. In Valhalla the best warriors –' Lotta mimed whacking someone with her sword – 'wait until they're needed at the end of the world.'

'That's not soon, is it?'

Lotta shrugged. 'That kind of depends on the Frost Giants.'

Whetstone tore his eyes away from the building of spears and shields. 'I thought it would be bigger.'

'It is, on the inside.'

Whetstone swallowed.

'I'm in training, I'm a Class Three,' Lotta continued, picking at her wrist guards. 'It was my first trip to Midgard. I was supposed to bring back a Hero.'

'But how did you find me? I was –' he paused, not wanting to admit what he had really been up to – 'nowhere near a battle.'

Lotta rolled her eyes. 'We got a bit lost, if you must know. And I couldn't come back empty-handed, so I brought –' she gestured at Whetstone – 'you.'

Whetstone gaped at her.

The girl looked at him critically. 'It's a shame you're not dead. Even if you weren't a Hero, I could've got away with it if you had been dead, but . . . So you have to go.'

'I don't see what the big deal is about Heroes anyway,' Whetstone huffed. 'Just because they have big muscles and cheese for brains.'

'Like you would know. You're nothing like a Hero.'

'Exactly. I don't have cheese for brains, and that's why I'm not going anywhere.' Whetstone grinned, his eyes bright. 'Think of the stories they would make up about me if I brought back proof that I'd been to Asgard.'

'Keep dreaming.' Lotta glowered at him. 'The only place you're going is back to Midgard. Now.'

'How?' Whetstone's stomach flipped in excitement. He jerked a thumb at Sleipnir. 'Maybe I could take him?'

'Yeah, steal Odin's horse. Really subtle. Why not borrow Freyja's Falcon Cloak or Loki's Sky-Walking Shoes and fly down?'

'Have *you* got flying shoes?'

'Not shoes, no.' Lotta straightened her shoulders. 'Come with me.'

❀

Whetstone found himself smuggled into yet another stable. Lotta had convinced Broken Tooth to stay outside and keep watch, just in case anyone came near.

These horses were bigger and more intimidating than anything found on a normal Viking farm. A large bay horse whinnied and pawed at the ground, flashing razor-sharp horseshoes.

Whetstone swallowed nervously. He wasn't used to horses; the Angry Bogey had only been interested in wolves.

'I'd like to hear more about these flying shoes,' Whetstone called, edging past the bay horse. 'Are they made of feathers or what? Cos feathers on the feet could be quite tickly.'

'Forget about the shoes. We're using the horses.' Lotta pulled herself up into her saddle. Thighbiter immediately swung around to try and take a lump out of her leg. Lotta yanked hard on his reins and the horse danced sideways in annoyance.

'Hey!' Whetstone's head popped up next to Thighbiter. 'You nearly squashed me.'

'Stop talking and get on!' Lotta reached down to pull him up on to the horse when a warning growl came from Broken Tooth.

'Oh no!' Lotta pushed Whetstone back into the straw. The boy landed with a crash. He opened his mouth to wheeze a complaint but fell silent as voices approached from outside.

'Are you sure this is where he said to wait?'

'You heard the message too. What's that?'

'Yergh, it's that slobbering dog of Lotta's. What's SHE doing here?'

'Hide!' Lotta hissed.

Looking around, Whetstone spotted a broad wooden

beam, which crossed the width of the stable roof. Quickly he reached up, pulling himself on to it, his boots disappearing just as two pale girls walked in. They spotted Lotta and came to a halt.

'Oh. It's you,' said one girl with a toss of her head. 'I thought the smell was the dog, but it's not.' Whetstone peered down and saw that the girls were identical – they must be twins, except one had half of her hair cut off at the shoulder, leaving her with one long silver plait and one short tuft. He sniggered into his sleeve.

The other girl laughed. 'Shouldn't you be off polishing armour, barnacle-breath?'

'Yeah, how many boots did Scold tell you to clean after your mess-up last week with the *Saga of Svenson the Selfish*?'

Below him, Lotta's knuckles cracked as they squeezed Thighbiter's reins.

'Ahem.'

Whetstone turned his head to see a tall woman squinting at them from the doorway. It shouldn't be possible to peer down your nose at someone who is sitting on a horse and is therefore much higher than you. The woman managed it, however. It was the same woman who had been looking for Broken Tooth after his dog-hair-in-Valhalla incident. 'What are you up to?' She glared at Lotta and the twins. 'You three should be helping serve mead in Valhalla.'

'We were just bringing some apples to Stinging Trots and Crashing Bore,' the first girl simpered. 'To say thank you for helping us on our trip to Midgard.' She held out an apple to the large bay horse who had tried to terrorize Whetstone.

'You made a good start, girls,' the woman boomed, her face turning red from the volume. 'Bringing back dead Heroes to fill Valhalla is every Valkyrie's ULTIMATE PURPOSE!'

Dust rained down from the roof. Whetstone gripped his beam tightly, ignoring the spider trying to climb into his ear.

Scold plucked the gate key off its hook. 'If you work hard, you can join the Class Twos later for extra flying practice. Until then, I expect to see you all in Valhalla.'

There was an excited yelp from outside – Broken Tooth had clearly been listening.

'Not you, Broken Tooth. We've only just finished cleaning

up from last time. You have five minutes.' The woman gave Lotta one last glare, before stomping away.

Lotta slumped in her saddle. She glanced towards Whetstone's hiding place, weighing up what to do.

Whetstone gave her an innocent smile, keen for them all to leave so that he could go exploring. It wasn't often a Viking had the opportunity to visit Asgard – alive, anyway.

After a moment Lotta sighed and swung a leg over Thighbiter's back to dismount. Whetstone's grin widened.

'Stay here,' Lotta muttered out of the side of her mouth as she pretended to be adjusting Thighbiter's bridle. 'I'll be back as soon as I can – just don't GO anywhere or DO anything.'

The girl who wasn't missing half her plait moved forward to block Lotta's path. 'Who are you talking to, mollusc-face? It can't be your friends, because you don't have any.'

'Get out of my way, Flee,' Lotta growled, trying to step around her. 'Before Scold comes back looking for us.'

Flee crossed her arms and narrowed her eyes. 'You're hiding something – what have you done now?'

'Nothing.' Lotta's fingers curled into fists. 'Mind your own business.' Behind her, Thighbiter stamped his hooves.

The other girl joined her sister. 'Did you forget to sharpen the throwing axes again?'

'Or leave the doors to Valhalla open so that the ravens got in and pooed everywhere?'

'Or brought back a zero instead of a Hero?'

Whetstone pulled the spider out of his ear and dropped it

on to Flee's head. He watched in satisfaction as it burrowed into her hair.

'SHUT UP!'

The one with the missing plait pushed a finger against Lotta's breastplate, poking her. 'Listen, scallop-brains – Flee and I are going to be head Valkyries one day, then things will change around here.' She poked Lotta again. 'You will never be a proper Valkyrie, you pathetic. Little. WHELK.'

Lotta glared back, her impatience growing. 'Watch out, Flay, or you might lose another plait.'

Flay snarled and moved to grab Lotta's arm, but Lotta dodged out of the way.

Behind them, the stable door slammed open, making the girls jump. Whetstone gripped the beam tightly to stop himself from falling off in shock.

'IF YOU ARE QUITE FINISHED!' boomed Scold. The mighty Valkyrie stood framed in the doorway, her massive horny helmet sparkling in the sunlight. 'I don't know what you three are up to, but it stops now. If you two –' she gestured at the twins – 'want to mess around in the stables, you can start by tidying the place up.' She thrust a broom at Flee, who took it reluctantly. 'Lotta, get into Valhalla NOW!'

Lotta walked towards the door, definitely *not* looking at the boy lying on the wooden beam. Luckily for him, no one had yet noticed he was there.

Flay's fingers flexed as Lotta walked past. Flee stuck out the broom to try and trip her up, but Lotta sidestepped it and headed out.

Whetstone loosened his grip on the splintery wood and lay back on his beam. When he'd agreed to steal Awfulrick's awful magic cup, he never thought he'd end up in another one of the Nine Worlds. Now he was trapped in Asgard in a stable full of flying horses with a bunch of very grouchy Valkyries. He brushed a spider web out of his hair. The magic cup might have to stay hidden for a little while longer. Whetstone grinned, thinking of all the other treasures in Asgard he could bring home with him.

Fortune and Glory awaits!

Chapter Seven

A Very Dodgy Warrior

Dust motes floated past Whetstone's nostrils, twinkling in the sunlight as he fought down a sneeze. He rubbed his nose and peered over his beam. Flee and Flay were in no hurry to leave the stables, and until they left, Whetstone was stuck, no matter how keen he was to get out and explore Asgard. It still didn't seem possible that he was really here. He pinched himself on the arm, just to check if he was dreaming. 'Ouch!'

One of the girls looked around. 'What was that?'

Whetstone froze, convinced that the noise had given him away. A shadow fell across the doorway.

'Oh it's you.' Flee tossed her plaits. 'We got your message. What do you want?'

'That's not very nice,' said the shadow.

Whetstone flinched. He recognized the voice – it belonged to Vali's father. Whetstone gripped on tightly to the beam. A thought occurred to him: if Vali's family live in Asgard, would that make Vali a God too? Vali: God of Stroppiness and an Unhealthy Interest in Knives. Whetstone wondered who Vali's dad might be. There were loads of Norse Gods, and Whetstone had never really bothered to pay attention to their stories, even though the Angry Bogey had demonstrated an unusual interest in their comings and goings. It was not as if he had ever expected to find himself face to face with one of them.

Holding his breath, Whetstone cautiously leaned over the beam to try and get a glimpse of what was happening below.

The light dimmed, then brightened as the figure stepped through the stable door. 'I was just checking up on my two favourite people.'

Flee sniffed. 'Yeah, right.'

'Where've you been?' Flay said sulkily. 'I missed your stories.'

'And where's the set of ivory runes you promised us after we found out where Frigg's magic cup was?'

'Yeah, it wasn't easy getting Frigg's servant to tell us.'

'I can't believe she sent it to Krud.' Flee sniggered. 'What a dump. What did you want it for, anyway? I'm sure there are easier ways to find out the future.'

Whetstone gripped on to the beam, unable to believe that Awfulrick's magic cup really belonged to the Goddess Frigg. Light Finger was right – it could tell the future.

'Wait,' Flay said slowly. 'Did you get in trouble again?'

'I'm hurt you would think such a thing,' the shadow purred as he approached the girls. 'I've just been visiting family.'

Flay fiddled with her plait. 'Where *is* Vali?'

Flee glared at her sister.

'Oh, you know Vali. He'll be lurking around somewhere.'

Flay giggled.

Whetstone craned his neck as the man passed under his beam. He saw a flash of golden hair, before a wooden post blocked his view.

'So what's been going on here?' The shadow sidled closer to the two girls. 'Nice haircut, Flay,' he added with a snicker.

'It's all Lotta's fault!' she wailed.

'Lotta?'

'You know, the one with the stinky dog!'

'She's a Class Three Valkyrie, like us.'

'For now.'

'Yeah.'

'She always ruins everything,' Flee complained. 'Last week she got thrown off her horse when we were practising our attack formation.'

'Then she forgot the words to *Svenson the Selfish* when we were performing in front of ALL of Valhalla,' Flay said with a sniff.

'Yeah, she called him Svenson the *Shellfish*!'

'And now she's brought a dodgy warrior back from the battle.'

Whetstone gripped the beam tightly, his palms suddenly clammy.

'Dodgy?' the man asked. 'How?'

Flee glanced at her sister. 'Well, you know we're supposed to bring back the best warriors? So most of us went for the big, burly ones covered in blood and scars. I even managed to get a Berserker, and they're nuts!'

'Berserk,' the man agreed.

Flee crossed her arms. 'But not Lotta. She turns up back at Asgard with this funny-looking boy – he wasn't even wearing any armour.'

'I don't think he was a real Hero.' Flay put her hands on her hips.

'I don't think he was a real Viking!' Flee snorted.

'We'll never get made Class Twos with her slowing us down,' Flay added. 'I mean, I got Yorick the Snot Muncher. YORICK THE SNOT MUNCHER, for Thor's sake! Who did she bring back? Wagner the Weedy?'

'Dagfin the Drip?'

'Bjorn the Boring?'

Whetstone tried very hard not to be offended. He plucked a fat earwig from a nearby joist and dropped it on to Flee's head. He might not be a Hero, but that was just rude.

'Where was the battle?' the man asked. Whetstone could hear the urgency in his voice.

Flee twitched as the earwig scrambled down her plait and tucked itself inside her collar. 'Dunno. Everywhere down there looks the same to me.'

'The Battle of Big Helmets – it was on the coast, two villages over from Krud. We were supposed to turn left at the cliffs, remember?' Flay gave her sister a funny look. 'Are you all right?'

Flee paused, pulling at her tunic. 'I'm fine. I just – Argh!' The fat earwig pinged out of her collar and launched itself towards Flay's face. Flay threw out her hand and batted it to the floor. She stamped down hard. Even Whetstone winced.

The man stepped forward. Whetstone could see the back of a tall, slender man wearing a fine red tunic. He leaned further out over the beam. 'What did Lotta's warrior look like?'

Flee let go of her collar and tossed her hair, one plait nearly hitting her sister in the face. 'He was young, like, our age. Weedy-looking. Blond hair. Kinda dirty, with a cloak.'

Flay sniggered, wiping her boot on the floor. 'Odin only knows where she got him from.'

'A stable, maybe?' the man asked. Whetstone felt like a trickle of ice had just run down his spine. This was bad. 'Did he have anything with him? The cup, perhaps?'

Flee wiped her hand on her skirt. 'Is that why you want him? You think he's got Frigg's cup?'

The man shifted, golden lights appearing in his hair. 'Maybe.' He straightened up. 'Did you see him enter Valhalla with the other Heroes?'

Flay crossed her arms. 'We didn't stick around to watch. I dropped mine off by the steps of Valhalla. Odin was there, so I assume they were all resurrected as usual.'

'Mine started to glow blue, like they're supposed to,' Flee added.

The man leaned forward. 'I would very much like to meet this mysterious boy, Hero or not. How about you find him for me? I suspect he never made it to Valhalla.'

Flay rolled her eyes. 'We don't work for you. We didn't get caught last time, but doing little favours for tricksters like you is against the Valkyrie code.'

The man turned, his sharp nose and collar-length hair silhouetted against the sunlight. 'I could make it worth your while.' He paused for a moment, then asked, 'Do you remember what happened when Sif got her hair cut off?'

'Yeah, by you, as a *joke*. It wasn't very funny.'

'Some people need to lighten up. Do you remember how I fixed it again?'

'You got the Dwarves to make her new hair out of gold.'

'And almost lost your head.'

The man waved the detail away as insignificant. 'I could do it again – replace that plait of yours with shining strands of living gold. Or in your case, silver.'

Flay's eyes widened. 'You'd do that – for me?'

He shrugged. 'Maybe. You see, what I like about you two girls is that you can see the bigger picture. Most people are caught up in the little details, but you're different. You can look ahead. And if you want to get ahead, it's useful to have friends who don't mind risking theirs.'

'You're weird, Loki.' Flee grinned.

Whetstone felt a pit open in his stomach. Loki! Vali's dad was Loki the Trickster. The Angry Bogey had loved to tell stories about Loki. About the trouble he had caused, and the terrible tricks he played against Gods and Giants.

'Just find me the boy,' Loki instructed.

'What are you going to do with him?'

Desperate to hear every word, Whetstone leaned dangerously far over the beam. Another spider climbed into his ear, and Whetstone shook his head, trying to knock it out. The movement left him unbalanced, his fingers slipping on the wood . . .

With a splintery *CRASH*, Whetstone tumbled off the beam and landed on the floor, right in between the twins. Clouds of dust and ancient horse droppings flew into the air. Whetstone felt like a tight band was fastening around his chest as he tried not to breathe in the foul stench.

Under their matching coatings of dust, Flee and Flay wore identical expressions of shock. Only Loki had escaped unscathed, having leaped out of the way in time.

Whetstone stared up into his handsome face. His scarred mouth was pulled into a laugh, but his eyes were dark and cold. 'Whetstone!'

Flee and Flay both screamed in unison.

'He's human!'

'He's alive!'

The two girls threw themselves towards the stable door. 'SCOOOOOOLLLLLLLDDDDDD!'

But before they could reach the door, a bright flash of green light filled the room. Whetstone flinched, remembering Loki's treatment of Vali. The girls' screams were abruptly cut off. Flee and Flay were motionless, encased in green light.

Their eyes and mouths open mid-scream. Their feet hanging in mid-air.

Loki turned away from them and pulled Whetstone to his feet in one easy movement. 'So you made it out of Krud, then,' he purred with a smile. 'And still alive – how surprising.'

Whetstone pulled himself away from the grinning man. 'What did you do to them?' He pointed at the twins.

'I froze them – I won't be needing them now.'

Whetstone backed away, deeper into the stables. 'How do you know my name? What did Vali tell you?'

'I don't need Vali to find things out.' Loki smiled more broadly, the scars stretching his lips, and Whetstone vaguely remembered a particularly gruesome story about Loki having his mouth sewn shut. 'You would be amazed at the things I know about you.'

Whetstone tried not to stare.

'I know you grew up in Drott.' Loki inched closer. 'And I know you long to be more than just the unremarkable child you are.' The man crept forward on silent feet. 'I know *you*, Whetstone, and I know you are in big trouble if anyone catches you – are you aware of what happens to living humans who come to Asgard?'

Whetstone didn't trust himself to speak. He shook his head.

'Niflheim.'

Whetstone was confused. 'What's Snifflheim?'

'No! Niflheim,' snapped Loki. 'You'll spend the rest of eternity in the land of the mist and shadows.'

'Oh, I thought you said Snifflheim – like the land of sniffles and drippy noses.'

'I don't think you understand the graveness of the situation you are in,' Loki hissed. His shape blurred for a moment, then he regained his normal appearance.

Whetstone gaped before remembering that Loki was a shapeshifter. More memories of the Angry Bogey's stories flickered across Whetstone's mind. Loki was a liar and a shapeshifter, and very, VERY clever. It was never entirely clear to Whetstone why the Gods let Loki stay in Asgard with them. He wasn't a God himself but a Fire Giant, and therefore able to do certain types of magic, but he always seemed to be getting into trouble. Whetstone gulped – he had thought Awfulrick was dangerous.

Whetstone tried not to blink. It was a bit like trying to outstare a snake. His eyes started to water.

The Trickster smiled. 'Now, you're lucky you ran into me. You see, I don't care why you're here or who brought you.'

A flicker of guilt ran across Whetstone's face as he thought of Lotta. He took a step backwards.

'All I want is the magic cup of Awfulrick, and I know you have it.'

Whetstone backed into a corner, the heels of his boots meeting the wall behind him. 'You mean the magic cup of Frigg? Can it really tell fortunes?' he asked, eyeing the doorway over Loki's shoulder.

Loki smiled again, his pale face floating out towards

Whetstone in the gloom. 'Indeed – it can tell the future of anyone who holds it.'

'Really?' Whetstone leaned forward. 'Does that mean the riddle has something to do with my future?'

The man's eyes widened in surprise, then narrowed again. 'Now wherever did you hear about a riddle?'

'I haven't – I just—' Whetstone protested. His words were cut short as the stable door creaked open. A shape stepped inside, too small for Scold, too few legs for Broken Tooth.

'Whetstone?' Lotta whispered.

The boy tried to call out, but Loki moved faster. In a tumble of feathers, a hawk appeared where the man had been and dived towards Lotta. Loki reformed, slipping in between Lotta and the stable door, closing it firmly behind her. She flinched and instinctively unsheathed the sword strapped across her back.

'Well, well. Look what I found,' Loki began in a sing-song voice, his face glowing eerily in the green light surrounding Flee and Flay. 'The thief and the Valkyrie – how sweet.'

Whetstone felt his face burn as Lotta lowered her sword and glowered at Loki. He slid into Thighbiter's stall. The horse sniffed him and tried to take a bite out of his hair.

'What are you talking about?' Lotta pointed at Flee and Flay with her sword. 'Scold sent me to fetch them.' She examined Flay, frozen mid-scream, and tried to give her a poke. 'Ow!' She sucked at her stinging fingers. 'You'd better unfreeze them. Scold wants them in Valhalla.'

The man laughed. 'I don't think you really mean that.'

'No?'

'You should be thanking me.' He edged Lotta deeper into the stables.

'Thanking you, Loki? For freezing Flee and Flay? I could've taken care of them myself.'

Loki just smiled his twisted smile. 'I know your little secret, Valkyrie girl. And now I'm the only thing standing between you and banishment from Asgard.'

Even in the green light, Whetstone could see Lotta's dark skin break out in a sweat. 'Banishment?' she croaked.

Loki nodded. 'Isn't that the punishment for breaking the Valkyrie code?'

Lotta swallowed. 'I don't know what you're talking about.' She sounded confident, but her shaking hands made her wrist guards rattle.

'Oh really?' Loki grinned. 'Then who is this? He doesn't look much like a dead Hero to me.'

Whetstone felt his body rise into the air as though he had been picked up by a gigantic hand. He cried out in shock, trying to grab hold of Thighbiter and failing. He floated away from the horse and hung suspended in front of Lotta, his toes dangling a foot above the ground.

Lotta gulped.

'You are very lucky, really,' Loki continued as Whetstone spun gently in the air. 'I happen to know that before he was brought to Asgard, this boy stole a magic cup. All he has to do is give it to me and I will make this whole thing –' he waved

his hand and Whetstone dropped to the floor with a bump – 'disappear.'

'I've never seen him before,' Lotta quavered.

'Oh dear,' Loki said. 'I hope you're not going to make this difficult.' The man opened his arms wide. 'I'm only trying to help,' he said, moving away. 'All I want is the cup. Of course, if you *want* to give up your Valkyrie powers and move to Midgard, I guess I could send Flee and Flay to tell Scold now?'

Lotta shook her head.

'Just leave her out of this,' called Whetstone, pushing his cloak out of his face.

Loki moved closer, his eyes fixed on the dark-haired Valkyrie. 'There's no need for Scold to ever know about your little mistake – as long as I get what I want.'

'I'm not a thief.' Lotta clenched her hands into fists.

'And you won't be a Valkyrie for much longer, either.'

Lotta took a deep breath and closed her eyes. She poked the boy with the toe of her boot. 'Go on then. Give it to him.'

Whetstone crossed his arms. 'No.'

Lotta opened her eyes. 'What do you mean, no?'

'He's not getting it. I have plans for that cup.'

'Don't be stupid!' Lotta pulled at his cloak, searching for pockets. 'Just give him the cup!'

Whetstone swatted her away. 'Tough luck – I don't have it with me!'

Loki looked like he had just bitten a lemon, an expression that reminded Whetstone a *lot* of Vali.

'But you know where it is,' Lotta hissed. 'Don't you?'

Whetstone bit the inside of his lip. He really didn't want to tell Loki what he had done with the cup, but Vali must have figured out it was somewhere on Ivor the Nose Grinder's farm. He needed to get there first . . . 'It's hidden on Midgard,' he said slowly, weighing his words.

Lotta turned to the handsome man. 'There you go – it's on Midgard. Whetstone will get it for you.'

Loki waved a hand towards Flee and Flay, and the magic holding them wavered.

'—OOOLLLD!' the twins wailed before freezing again.

'I'll go with him and bring it to you,' Lotta amended, her fingers twisting together. 'We'll give you the cup and we can all forget this ever happened. But what about Flee and Flay?' She gestured towards the eerie glow in the doorway. 'You can't keep them frozen forever.'

'Bring me the cup and I'll make sure they don't remember a thing, Gods' honour,' Loki replied, holding up three fingers in a kind of salute.

Lotta squinted at him.

'Think of it as a quest,' Loki continued, holding eye contact with Lotta. 'Worthy of Heroes.'

'Heroes,' Lotta murmured.

'Just one problem – as everyone keeps pointing out, I'm not a Hero.' Whetstone crossed his arms.

Lotta and Loki turned to look at him.

Whetstone glared at Loki. 'Even if I give you the cup, how do I know you'll keep your side of the bargain? You could still send me to Snifflheim or wherever.'

Loki focused his dark eyes on Whetstone, and the boy felt himself trapped in their penetrating gaze. 'I can give you everything you ever wanted . . . Fame and Fortune.' Loki ran his hand along the stable wall. His fingers left behind a trail of yellow sparks, which turned into golden coins. Whetstone's eyes grew wide as more money than he had ever seen in his life dripped on to the floor. 'Don't you want minstrels to sing songs about you?'

Whetstone paused, arguments dying in his throat.

Loki turned back to Lotta. 'Of course,' he added delicately, 'if the boy fails, I will be unable to prevent you from facing the punishment laid down by Odin and the Valkyrie council.'

Lotta's brow furrowed. 'So it all depends on him? That's not fair!'

'Life's not fair, Princess.'

Whetstone tried to keep his face blank as his mind spun. This *would* make a great story for the minstrels to sing about him. Visiting Asgard, making oaths, finding magical treasures was all good stuff. He dragged his eyes away from the piles of golden coins. But he would need something to prove he'd been there. And of course, just because he dug up the cup, it didn't mean he had to give it to Loki straight away. If the cup could tell the future, Whetstone had some questions he wanted it to answer first. Like, would he become the greatest thief EVER? Or, how could he get rid of that itchy rash behind his left knee? Of course, Light Finger would be upset about not getting the cup, but Whetstone felt he could find something here in Asgard to bring him instead.

'OK,' Whetstone said out loud. 'It's a deal. The cup for Fame and Fortune.'

Loki rubbed his hands together. 'Excellent! So that's decided then. You have one day to bring me the cup or I unfreeze the twins.'

Lotta looked up in panic. 'Wait a minute – one day? That's not very long.'

Loki smiled at her, the movement stretching his scars into strange shapes. 'No,' he agreed. 'It isn't.'

Chapter Eight

Trouble in the Tree

Whetstone's boots kicked up dust as he trailed along behind Lotta, keeping his eyes peeled for small, easily pocketable Asgardian trinkets. They had left the stables far behind them and were following the narrow twisting lanes deep into the heart of Asgard. Lotta had sent Broken Tooth home, a look of doggy disappointment on his face.

Whetstone shook his cloak over his shoulders, nearly dislodging the large orange-spotted spider that had tucked itself into a fold in the fabric. He ran a few steps to keep up with Lotta.

'I told you to stay in the stables,' the girl snorted as she marched along, her brown arms swinging stiffly.

'I did.'

'I told you to keep out of trouble.'

'Actually, you didn't.'

'But nooo! You have to get mixed up with Loki. *Loki* of all people, and now we're off on this stupid quest.'

'Wait a minute,' Whetstone argued, catching up with her. 'Don't go blaming me – you lot let Loki wander around unsupervised. Even I know he's trouble.'

'He's Odin's blood brother. And he gets us out of as much trouble as he gets us into.'

'Yeah, right.' After a moment, Whetstone added, 'So we're not using the horses then?'

'No, thanks to you. Scold took the key that opens the gateway.'

'So how else are we going to get down? I should've asked Loki about his flying shoes.'

Lotta snorted.

'What's your problem? I thought you wanted me to go back to Midgard.'

'I do, but handling stolen goods isn't exactly Valkyrie-like.'

'You need to stop being so full of yourself. If I hadn't stolen the cup, you wouldn't have anything to make a deal with.'

Lotta spun on her heels. 'I cannot believe I am stuck with you! How could I have thought, even for an instant, that you were a Hero?'

Whetstone felt the heat rise in his face. 'Maybe it's because you're not a very good Valkyrie!'

Lotta's hands curved into fists. 'I am not being banished because of YOU!' Whetstone was surprised to see her hands were shaking. 'Just – get the cup, OK? And then we can pretend none of this ever happened.' She clomped off.

The buildings were thinning out now. Ahead of them, Whetstone could see a wide expanse of trees. Lotta paused on the edge of the forest and kicked at a clump of grass, sending a butterfly fluttering.

Whetstone joined her at the tree line. The forest seemed to be entirely made of fruit trees; he spotted apples, pears and plums hanging thickly on the branches. Each one ripe, juicy and *golden*. Whetstone's mouth watered and his fingers itched to touch them. One of those would be perfect to prove that he'd been to Asgard. If he did have to give up the cup, lots of people would like to hear this story instead, and Light Finger would love a golden apple. He reached out a hand . . .

'Stop right there.' Lotta whacked him on the arm. 'Those aren't for you. Gods only.'

'Temper, temper.' Whetstone rubbed his arm. 'Where are we, anyway?'

'This is Idunn's orchard.'

'And we're here because?'

Lotta gave a half-smile. 'Because we're going to climb.'

'Climb?'

'Yes. Down that.' She stopped in front of the most enormous tree Whetstone had ever seen, so wide a dozen men couldn't have circled it with linked arms. Its branches disappeared high above into the clouds. The trunk sank into the earth, somehow passing through the ground.

Whetstone gaped. 'That's . . . That's . . .'

'Yggdrasil, the world tree.' Lotta touched the trunk. 'Midgard – the human world where you SHOULD be, where the CUP is – is down. All we have to do is climb.'

Whetstone stared, wide eyed. 'Climb down the world tree? Can you even do that?'

Lotta shrugged. 'I don't know anyone who's tried, but I don't see why we can't.' She grabbed a low branch and swung herself out on to the tree. 'Come on, lazybones. We've only got one day.'

Feeling Lotta's eyes burning into him, Whetstone turned reluctantly away from the golden apples. If the apples were out, he would just have to make sure he had a go with the cup before Loki got his hands on it.

Whetstone straightened his cloak, and the orange-spotted spider used its sticky web to attach itself more securely to the rough fabric. With a sigh, he reached for the nearest branch.

❦

They had barely made it through the cloud layer, and Whetstone's arms and legs already ached. The enormous size of the tree made it difficult to find footholds and handholds. The branches were as thick as a man's body and widely spaced. Large green leaves waved lazily in the breeze, threatening to send Whetstone tumbling into the abyss below. He rubbed his hands together and flexed his fingers. The damp clouds had made him chilly, and his clothes were beginning to stick to him uncomfortably.

Far, far below them was Midgard. It sat wedged between Yggdrasil's trunk and a thick branch. Water cascaded endlessly over the world's edges. It was very beautiful, but it made him feel a bit sick to see the islands and seas spread out like that. He was used to standing on Midgard, not looking at it.

'They climbed down the great world tree . . .' Whetstone began, pulling his eyes from the far-away world and reaching for a nearby branch.

> They climbed down the great world tree,
> It was a sight for anyone to see,
> I trust they won't slip,
> So keep a good grip,
> And hope you don't need to pee!

He sniggered to himself and carefully hooked an arm around the next branch.

'What are you grinning about?' Lotta called from above.

Whetstone looked up at her.

'How can you tell I'm grinning?'

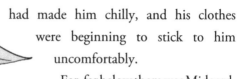

'I just can. Now stop putting me off.' Lotta tightened her grip on the smooth bark. 'This is harder than it looks.'

Lotta was not having an easy time climbing down Yggdrasil. Her boots were heavy, covered in metal studs and leather straps: perfect for kicking your enemy when they were on the ground; not so good for climbing down slippery tree branches. 'I cannot believe I'm going to Midgard again – twice in one day.'

'You never know – you might get to like it,' Whetstone teased. 'It's not so bad really.'

'Ha.'

Wedging himself in the fork of a particularly wide branch, Whetstone paused for a breather. He brushed leaves out of his hair and wiped a hand across his face. 'Any idea how long this is going to take?'

'No. Just keep going.'

Whetstone shook his aching arms. Thieving wasn't usually so tiring – except for when you were being chased, of course. He sat down on the branch, his legs dangling. After a moment, Lotta sighed and copied him.

'Listen, I'm sorry for – kidnapping you, in Krud.' Lotta took off her helmet and rubbed her forehead where the metal pinched her. 'I really did think you were dead.'

'Dead?'

'You were lying unmoving on the floor. It wasn't until we were at the gates of Asgard and you started snoring that I realized. By then it was too late.' Lotta raked her fingers through her black curls, which were starting to go frizzy from the damp clouds.

'I don't snore!'

'I was so shocked, I thought I was going to fall off Thighbiter!' Lotta giggled, looking much friendlier. 'I'm sorry.' She bit her lip. 'I needed someone – I was desperate.'

'Thanks.'

'I didn't mean it like that.' She spun the helmet around in her hands. 'You heard what our teacher Scold said: *Bringing back dead Heroes to fill Valhalla is every Valkyrie's Ultimate Purpose.* I don't think she'd be impressed to find out I got a mangy thief instead.'

'Oi, I am not mangy!' Whetstone leaned back on his arms. 'I still don't understand why you're all obsessed with Heroes.'

'How else are we going to keep the Frost Giants away?'

'Dunno, maybe you could try asking someone who doesn't have cheese for brains?'

Lotta gave him a shove. 'Even if you were a Hero – which you're not – you're not dead. That's kind of important.'

'I'll be dead one day though, so maybe you're just early?'

Lotta looked doubtful. 'I don't think Scold will buy that.'

'Won't she be looking for you? And those two other girls in the stables?'

Lotta scraped her curls back into place. 'Hopefully Loki can distract her for a bit.'

'What did he do to those girls? Will they be OK?'

'Looked like a freezing spell. It's so unfair – I wish I could do magic.'

'Can't you?'

'No. Only Dwarves, Giants and Elves can do magic.'

Whetstone glanced sideways at Lotta. 'So Valkyries aren't magic then? You've got a flying horse!'

Lotta shook her head. 'We're not magic ourselves. We can generate magic from performing Heroic acts and use that to give ourselves powers, like long lives, extra strength, animal transformations.'

'Animal transformations?'

Lotta rubbed her nose. 'Traditionally Valkyries can turn into swans.'

'I saw someone do that! Back in Asgard, one minute there was a girl, the next minute a bird,' Whetstone exclaimed.

'That must've been Akrid, she's a Class Two and is always showing off,' Lotta huffed. 'Just because she got one hundred per cent in her animal transformations, she doesn't have to brag about it.'

'Whetstone smirked at Lotta's grumpy expression, then something caught his eye. 'Hey, what's that?' He gestured at something over Lotta's shoulder.

Lotta peered around, then turned back. 'It's the branch that leads to the Elves. Look, you can see the sign: *Alf-heim* means "Elf-Home". It's a place we do not need to go right now.'

'No, not the sign – that sparkly gold stuff.' Whetstone shuffled past her towards the branch.

Lotta yanked on the edge of his cloak. 'Will you just leave it? Whatever it is, it's not for you.'

Whetstone shrugged her off and dropped down a couple of branches to reach the one with the sign. A short distance along the branch sat the source of the light. It was a shimmering golden harp, half covered with a pile of leaves. It was about as long as Whetstone's arm and slightly triangular in shape, with a curved figurehead like those found on ships. 'It's a harp. Why's there a harp in Yggdrasil?'

Lotta dropped down next to him with a thud. 'Maybe one of the Elves lost it? They're a bit scatterbrained.'

Whetstone's fingers itched to touch the harp – something like that would definitely get all the minstrels singing about him. He dropped on to his knees and reached out a hand.

'I wouldn't if I were you.'

Whetstone rolled his eyes. 'You are a right misery guts, has anyone ever told you that?'

Lotta marched past him, the branch bouncing slightly under her feet. She pointed up into the branches over the harp. 'Look, dummy – it's a trap.' Hanging over the harp was a finely woven net, half hidden in the leaves. 'It's obviously there to catch anyone who tries to touch the harp.'

Whetstone lowered his arm. 'Do lots of people use Yggdrasil to get around?'

Lotta sniffed. 'No, not really.'

'So why stick a harp out here and why bother with a trap?'

'Dunno. But it's the sort of thing the Dwarves make, and they get really touchy if you start fiddling with their stuff.'

Whetstone nodded. He inched closer to the harp. 'Ouch!' Tears sprang to his eyes. A large orange-spotted spider had just sunk his fangs into his hand. Whetstone shook his hand, sending the spider tumbling.

Lotta watched him with a bit of a smirk on her face. 'Is that a friend of yours?'

'It just bit me! I hope it wasn't poisonous.' Whetstone sucked the bite mark.

'It's braver than me. I wouldn't want to bite you. I might catch something.'

'Ha, ha.'

Lotta grinned. 'Maybe it just doesn't like harp music?'

Whetstone peered up at her. 'Do they teach you jokes as part of your Valkyrie training? Because if they do, you're definitely going to fail.'

Lotta stuck her tongue out.

Whetstone slid on to his stomach. 'There's something carved into the frame.' He paused, peering at Lotta over his shoulder. 'If the net falls, are you going to pull me out?'

Lotta snorted and crossed her arms.

'I'm the only one who knows where the cup is,' he reminded her.

Lotta tossed her head. 'Fine. Although I don't see why you can't leave it alone. It's clearly enchanted. It might make you turn into a monster, or make you fall asleep for a hundred years, or you might start speaking backwards or something.'

'It must be important, otherwise why set a trap?' Whetstone grinned. 'Anyway, I'm not going to take it – I just want to see what it says.'

'Yeah, right.'

Lotta glared as Whetstone slid forward on his belly, the branch quivering under him. He glanced upward; the net trembled slightly in the breeze. Whetstone stretched out an arm, his fingertips just brushing against the harp frame.

Behind him, Lotta sighed and snapped off a leaf from a nearby branch. 'Here, use this.' She passed it to him. 'I can't believe I'm helping you.'

'See, being a thief isn't so bad.'

'I think I prefer Heroes.'

Carefully Whetstone stretched out the leaf, knocking the harp on its side. The net shivered above him. Gulping, he painstakingly hooked the leaf through the hole in the centre of the harp and dragged it closer.

Sitting up, Whetstone twisted the wooden frame around in his hand – it was smooth and curiously warm. His fingers traced over fractures and breaks in the wood. The frame had once been carved out of a single piece of wood, but at some point it had been broken into pieces, then stuck back together again.

'Maybe someone is hiding it because it's broken?' Lotta suggested.

'I don't think so.' The harp frame sparkled in the sunlight. Carved into one side of it were the words *Skera: I cut*. 'I cut? That is a pretty weird thing to be written on a harp. Music can't cut, can it?'

'Depends how badly you play it.' Lotta shuddered. 'Just put it back and let's get out of here. That harp is giving me the creeps.'

'Fine, but I'm sure I've heard something about the Skera Harp before . . .'

'I'm sure you talk about it all the time with your thief friends.'

'No . . .' Whetstone said slowly, tracing the letters with his fingers and trying to remember. 'I heard it somewhere else.'

Lotta stooped forward and tried to tug the wooden frame out of his hands.

'Hey!' Whetstone clung on.

Lotta yanked harder. 'Let go – we've got to put it back and get the cup!'

'Get off – you'll have us both over!' Whetstone pulled the harp out of Lotta's grasp. He stood up, clutching a nearby branch for support. 'It's just an old harp; I bet no one even wants it. Let me take it back to Midgard.'

'You have got to be joking!' Lotta lunged forward again. The branch wobbled beneath them.

'I told you I was a thief,' Whetstone retorted, swaying a little to try and avoid Lotta's grasping fingers. 'You want the cup for Loki, and you wouldn't let me take a measly apple. If I can't have the cup, I'm taking the harp. When I bring this back to Midgard, everyone in the Nine Worlds will know my name. You get the cup; I get the harp. Fair's fair.'

'You're doing all this because you want to be famous!?' She snatched at the harp. 'You total . . . complete . . . pillock!'

'Get off, it's mine.' Whetstone pulled the harp up out of her reach.

Lotta made a lunge for the harp. She overbalanced, her

arms windmilling furiously as she fought to stay upright. Her foot slipped off the branch and she slammed heavily into Whetstone, her waving arm knocking the shining harp from the boy's grasp. She frantically grabbed hold of his shirt to try and stop herself from falling.

Whetstone was yanked downward by Lotta's weight, his fingers scrabbling at the tree's bark, trying to find something to hold on to. His stomach rolled as the world swung sickeningly below him. His hand hit upon a smaller branch and he gripped it tightly. They hung together, swinging gently in the breeze.

Whetstone forced his eyes open and watched as the golden harp dropped down, down, DOWN.

'NO!' Shoving Lotta away, Whetstone heaved himself along the branch to try and catch it. That harp was his ticket to Fame and Fortune, and he was not giving up on it. He felt his body slip, his fingers desperately fumbling once again for purchase. Then there was only air beneath

him. Whetstone closed
his eyes.

He came to a
shuddering stop. One foot
caught in something. He hung
upside down, his cloak swinging
around his face. The orange-
spotted spider dangled
casually out of his collar,
ticking his nose. 'You again!'
Whetstone swiped it away
and it vanished into his cloak.

His heart hammering, he
risked a peek and saw Lotta's
grim face peering through
the leaves. She had landed
in the fork of a branch
and caught him, one hand
gripping his boot tightly. Whetstone
felt his foot slip.

'Stop wiggling,' Lotta muttered through gritted teeth.
'I'll drop you.'

Whetstone tried to hold his cloak away from his face.
There was a branch, just close enough to reach – maybe. He

stretched out an arm as Lotta's hand slipped on his boot. He tried to grip on with his toes.

'Over there,' he called, pointing at the branch. Lotta nodded, her head dipping through the leaves. He twisted, trying to turn his body towards the branch.

'After three,' called Lotta in a strained voice. 'One . . . Two . . .' Her grip slipped again. 'Three!' With a mighty heave, she swung the boy towards the tree branch and let go. He tumbled down with a crash of breaking branches.

Slowly Lotta parted the leaves with shaking fingers. 'Whetstone, are you all right?'

The tree shifted and creaked under her. A dirty and dishevelled head popped up. With a wave of relief, Lotta crawled along the branch and dropped down next to Whetstone. His face was red and blotchy from dangling upside down, but he laughed. Lotta laughed too, the panic pouring out of her. She rubbed her hands over her face and hiccupped a giggle, before turning serious.

'What happened to the harp?'

Chapter Nine

Dragons Are Not Morning People

The golden harp dropped down, down, DOWN. Crashing through leaves and bouncing through birds' nests. It snagged for a moment on a narrow branch before slipping free again. It fell past the fields and forests of Midgard, past the dark caves of the Dwarves, and onward into the mists below.

It tumbled along twisting roots, finally landing in a patch of grass with a *thunk*. It fell forward, knocking into something hard and unmoving.

The thing the harp had knocked into was large, scaly, and until just now had been asleep. But it is hard to sleep when something has rolled into your ear. The dragon, Nidhogg, opened one eye and looked around. He did not like mornings and was in no mood to deal with things hitting him on the head before he had even had breakfast.

Nidhogg dwelt in the land of Niflheim, the lowest and darkest of the Nine Worlds supported by Yggdrasil. It was flat and empty except for scrubby grass and endless swirling mist. Niflheim was the land of mist and shadow, one of two worlds that Vikings could find themselves in after death. Niflheim was the final destination of Vikings who had died in embarrassing or cowardly ways. There they roamed around telling each other lies about how great they had been when they were alive and getting lost in the endless mists.

Nidhogg was the only living thing in all of Niflheim, and he loved to terrorize the dead Vikings that were sent there. When he fancied a break from blowing fire at them or trying to whack them with his scaly tail, he would chew on the roots of the great world tree, hoping to bring the upper worlds crashing down. He was about the size of a small house, with dark red scales and distinctive fins that flared out around his head when he was annoyed. He uncoiled his long red tail and flicked it from side to side, sending a crowd of unworthy dead who had crept forward to check out the harp fleeing in terror.

Nidhogg lifted his scaly head and belched out a huge fireball. Looking around for the thing that had woken him, the dragon spotted the harp frame lying innocently in the patchy grass. The dragon aimed a gust of flame at the golden harp, intending to incinerate it and teach it a lesson. But instead of turning into ash, it glowed brightly. Nidhogg tried again, heating the harp until it glowed white hot. The dragon watched as it cooled slowly, emitting a faint *plink*ing noise, seemingly completely unharmed by the fire.

Dragons have excellent eyesight and very good hearing, and despite living in a world of mist and shadow, Nidhogg was no exception. So when he screwed up his yellow eyes and peered high up into Yggdrasil, although they were very far away indeed, the dragon could clearly see two tiny people.

Nidhogg puffed out some smoke and stretched his claws like a cat. The two little people might think it was funny to be throwing musical instruments at him now, but soon they would make an excellent snack.

The dragon started to climb.

Chapter Ten

The Wyrm

Whetstone retied his boot and tried to flatten his hair which stuck out in all directions. He glanced over at Lotta, who was peering down through the tree branches. Her face and arms were covered in scrapes from lunging through the branches after him. Her curls were full of leaves and twigs poked of out her armour.

Lotta looked back at him and giggled. 'You look like a scarecrow in a hurricane.'

'You should see you.' Whetstone wiped his face on his sleeve, clearing his throat guiltily. 'So, erm, thanks . . . for saving me.'

'I couldn't just let you fall.' Lotta wrapped a strip of cloth around her grazed palm, the fabric looking stark against her brown skin. 'I need you to find the cup. The good thing is, we're a lot closer to Midgard now.' Holding the cloth with her teeth, she fastened it into a knot. 'I hope none of the Dwarves come looking for their harp – Odin only knows where it's ended up.'

'But . . . I needed it.'

'Fame, Fortune and all that?'

'Well, yeah. A golden harp would definitely make me famous. I would be welcome at every Great Hall, I would get to sit up at the top table, and no one would throw chicken bones at me ever again.'

'So you want to be a thief to avoid chicken bones? Ha, you should see Valhalla on a Friday night. Or any night, really.'

'Not just that.' Whetstone shrugged one shoulder. 'I'd never make it as a fighter, or an explorer, or a, you know . . ."

'A Hero?'

Whetstone scratched his nose, leaving a smudge behind. 'But everyone likes stories. If I can give the world great stories, then everyone will know my name, and no one will care how I did it.'

'You sound like Loki.'

'No I don't!' the boy replied hotly.

'Yes, you do.' Lotta giggled. 'Being a trickster might be impressive, but it doesn't make you nice.'

'Being a thief is better than being a nobody.' Whetstone pouted. 'Haven't you ever wished to be someone you're not?'

Lotta screwed up her nose, her dark eyebrows knitting together in thought. 'No – not really,' she said at last. 'Valkyries are created out of pure battle frenzy and brought to life by the breath of Odin. Odin created me specifically to be a Valkyrie. Maybe you just need to figure out who you are meant to be.'

Whetstone leaned forward, hunching his shoulders. 'It's not that easy. You've got people to help you – I'm an orphan.

117

It's always just been me, on my own.'

'It that why you're so smelly? No parents around to make you take a bath?' Lotta teased.

'That's not true,' the boy countered with a bit of a grin. 'I had a bath last month.' (Actually, it hadn't been a bath. Whetstone had been caught trying to pick pockets in the Great Hall of Arne the Atrocious. They had thrown him out of the village and into a pond.)

Lotta poked him with her toe. 'Did you ever try finding them? I mean, most humans do have parents, don't they?'

The boy shrugged. 'I tried, but no one seems to know where I came from. I just turned up one day, in a basket in the centre of the village.'

Lotta tipped her head. 'What was in the basket with you?'

'What do you mean?'

'Maybe there was a clue to your identity – like a sword or a piece of jewellery – or perhaps a detailed letter explaining everything?'

Whetstone shook his head. 'No, nothing. Just me, wrapped in a blanket.'

Lotta wrinkled her nose. 'Well, I doubt that's a clue.'

'The village elders gave me to my foster mother – I call her the Angry Bogey. She runs a home for orphaned wolf cubs. I dunno why they thought she would want to take care of me. She's not interested in anything that doesn't have four legs and a tail.' Whetstone picked at his grubby fingernails. 'So you see, back in Drott I was never going to be anybody other than Whetstone the Nobody.'

'Whetstone the Chew Toy . . . Whetstone the Flea-Bitten.'

Whetstone coughed loudly to stop her talking. 'But then I met Light Finger.'

'Who's Light Finger? Is he important?'

'Seriously, you've never heard of Light Finger? He's the Greatest Thief in All the Known World!'

Lotta shrugged.

Whetstone eyed her in amazement. 'Well, Light Finger turned up in Drott one day. He told me I could be his apprentice. He said he would teach me everything he knew about thieving and that one day *I* could be the Greatest Thief in the Known World.'

'He told you to steal the magic cup?'

The boy nodded. 'That's what I was doing in the stable when you found me. I'd taken the cup and was hiding from Chief Awfulrick.'

Lotta screwed up her face. 'But how did Loki know that *you* – no offence – stole it?'

Whetstone looked at her sideways. 'Because when I met Light Finger, Vali was with him.'

Lotta gasped, her eyes wide. 'Vali? Like, Loki's son Vali? Ridiculously pale, likes knives, bit creepy?'

Whetstone nodded. 'I think Loki must have sent him to get the cup.'

Lotta shuddered. 'I wouldn't want to be in Vali's shoes when Loki found out you took it instead.'

Remembering the flashes of green light he had seen in the house, Whetstone shook his head.

'I mean, no one really likes Vali,' Lotta continued. 'Apart

from Flee and Flay, who have no taste, obviously. He's always skulking around with those knives. But we do feel a bit, you know, sorry for him.'

Whetstone nodded. 'Imagine having Loki as a dad – no wonder Vali always looks miserable.'

Lotta tapped her fingers on her knees. 'But *why* is everyone so desperate to get their hands on this cup? Are cups really rare in Midgard or something?'

Whetstone shrugged. 'The cup can talk. Loki said something about it telling me my future, and Light Finger thinks it will make us rich and famous. But when I had it, all it did was recite stupid poems.'

'So why is Loki interested in what happens in your future? I thought you said you weren't anyone important.'

'Thanks.'

'Sorry.' Lotta bit her lip. 'But you know what I mean – you're not a king or a great Hero or anything.'

Whetstone grinned. 'Not yet, anyway. Maybe I'm going to be a famous thief.'

'And we're back to the thieving.'

'It's not such a big deal.' Whetstone grinned. 'You're like my accomplice, now.'

Lotta's shoulders slumped; she ran her hands over her face. 'This is a nightmare,' she moaned. 'We have to get that cup. Loki means what he said. If we don't, Flee and Flay will tell Scold about us, and I'll be banished.'

'And I'll be sent to Snifflheim. Midgard doesn't sound so bad compared to that.'

Lotta looked at him. 'If I lose my Valkyrie powers and am sent to Midgard, I won't just turn into a human and get to live happily ever after. I'll be cursed to wander alone, never knowing victory again.' She sounded completely wretched. 'I know I'm a rubbish Valkyrie – I can't get the hang of Epic Poetry, and I'm more likely to stab myself than the enemy. But I'm literally made of the spirit of battle. It's my destiny to fight, whether I like it or not!'

Whetstone winced.

'What use is a Valkyrie who can't fight?' Lotta broke into sobs. 'And, worst of all, I'll – never – get to – see Broken Tooth again!'

Whetstone awkwardly patted her on the arm. Lotta sounded as miserable and alone as he was. 'C'mon, let's keep climbing down. We've still got time before those girls are unfrozen. And I don't suppose I'll get the harp back now.'

They both leaned forward, gazing through the branches hoping for a glint of gold.

Lotta wiped her face with the back of her hand. 'Can you hear that?'

Whetstone could just make out a faint sort of crunching, scraping noise. It was coming from below them.

'What do you think it is?' he asked, looking at Lotta. But she wasn't looking at him – her brown eyes were wide and staring at something half hidden by the leaves. Branches rustled and shifted as something climbed up the tree. Something large. A flash of red scales and a pointed tail appeared for a moment. Whetstone sat back, his heart pounding.

'It's the *Wyrm*,' Lotta breathed.

Whetstone scrunched up his face. 'That's not a worm.'

'Not wOrm – *WYrm*,' she replied with emphasis.

'What's the difference?'

'One is a small creature that lives in the dirt. The other is a massive fire-breathing serpent that's going to EAT US!' Lotta looked around desperately, 'That's Nidhogg. How did he get this far up Yggdrasil? We're not even at Midgard yet!'

'Nidhogg?'

'Do you not know *anything*? You should read this some time.' She thrust the crumpled *Guide to the Nine Worlds* into his hands.

Whetstone glanced at it. 'Now really isn't quiet reading time.'

Lotta tossed her head. 'Nidhogg lives in Niflheim, down there.' She pointed down the trunk of Yggdrasil. 'For him to have climbed up this far, he must be really angry.' She looked pointedly at Whetstone. 'I'll give you three guesses why.'

Whetstone's stomach did a flip, remembering the harp crashing through the branches. 'Why don't you just say *dragon*, like normal people?'

'It is part of the Valkyrie training. It's called speaking EPICALLY – like you're a Hero in a Saga.'

'Gotcha.' Whetstone tore his eyes away from the red scales and curved claws. 'So what are we going to do?'

Lotta looked at him. 'Like it or not, you've got to be a Hero now!'

'Fight *that*? You have got to be kidding!'

'Why not? Heroes are good at getting rid of dragons. Have your brains turned to cheese yet?'

'No way! I thought Valkyries were supposed to perform Heroic acts – you do it!'

The dragon was gaining steadily. In a few minutes it would reach them. It had the advantage of LONG SHARP CLAWS to dig into the tree bark to give it extra grip. Whetstone tried not to think about those claws digging into *him*. It was climbing much faster than they could, so there was no point in going up, and going down was out of the question – that would just mean being eaten sooner.

'Does it say anything in your guidebook about dragons?' Whetstone peered at the tattered paper. 'Have you got anything gold?' He checked his pockets. The orange-spotted spider came out clinging to the boy's finger. He pulled it off his hand carefully to avoid the fangs and tossed it away. It drifted away from them on the breeze, clutching a shimmering strand of silk.

Lotta rolled her eyes. 'Yes – let me just find my *golden* sword, and my *golden* armour and all the *golden* coins I always carry around with me.'

'I'm serious – it says here he loves gold. I thought maybe we could distract him with something.'

Lotta smirked. 'Are you thinking like a Hero?'

'This isn't Heroism – it's survival! And I don't see you coming up with any ideas.' Whetstone sulked, shoving the guidebook into his pocket. 'I bet those girls in the stable would think of something. What are you going to do, speak to it EPICALLY?' Whetstone cleared his throat. '*O Nidhogg the Great and Wondrous, please say you're not going to eat us.*' He waved his arms about.

Lotta's face cleared. 'That's it! But I don't think I can . . .' She turned away and started muttering to herself, her face screwing up in concentration.

Heat and smoke rose through the branches, making Whetstone's damp hair and clothes steam. Sunlight gleamed off dark red scales.

Whetstone dug his fingernails into his palms. 'Whatever you're doing, you need to do it quicker.' He could clearly see long dagger-like claws and enormous yellow eyes with dark-slitted pupils. He shrank back against the tree trunk trying to look small and unappetizing.

Lotta crawled back to him. 'I need your help. I need you to –' she avoided his eyes – 'make up a poem about me.'

Whetstone goggled. 'What? You have got to be kidding!'

'No, seriously. Epic Poetry – it's one of the six key elements of Valkyrie training. Fighting, Horse Riding, Serving Mead, Collecting Fallen Warriors, Animal Transformation and Epic Poetry.'

Whetstone's mouth hung open.

'It doesn't have to be about me, I suppose. But my powers will be stronger if I'm mentioned.'

Whetstone just stared.

'What have you got to lose?' Lotta asked reasonably as the dragon crept closer. 'I need something to give my powers a boost, and we don't have a horse, or any mead. I suppose I could whack you with my sword?'

Whetstone shook his head.

'I'm rubbish at remembering the words to poems, so you'll have to do it. It's either this, or jumping and dying painfully, or being eaten and dying painfully.'

Whetstone swallowed, his throat dry and cracked. '*She brings a lot of scrapes and grazes,*' he tried. '*She is well and truly frightening . . .*'

Lotta smiled a strange smile, stood up and walked away from Whetstone towards the end of the branch.

'*She has got a scowly face. Please, Thor, don't hit me with your lightning!*' He quavered to a stop.

Lotta crossed her arms over her chest and looked up at the sky. Before Whetstone could stop her, she stepped backwards out into the open air. There was a flash of white-blue light and a loud *CRACK.* Lotta vanished.

In her place was a very large bird. It looked a bit like a swan, a bit like a duck. But only if you had never seen a swan or a duck before and were trying to make one up from your imagination.

Whetstone gawked. 'Lotta?'

The weird swan-duck thing nodded and gestured with its wing for him to approach.

The dragon was close now. So close Whetstone could feel its heat rising through his boots. A trickle of sweat ran down the side of his neck. Carefully he shuffled along the branch towards the bird. It really was an odd-looking thing. Half of its feathers seemed to be stuck on the wrong way. He cautiously reached out a hand. The bird flapped its wing, knocking him sideways. He clung to a branch, steadying himself. The bird nodded its head and waddled around on the branch. It seemed to be suggesting that Whetstone climb on its back.

Riding a large bird while halfway up a giant tree and about to be eaten by a dragon is not as easy as it sounds. It requires a particular set of skills – things like balance, grace and confidence. Skills that, as it turned out, Whetstone didn't have. If Whetstone had really been a Viking Hero, he would have simply leaped into the air, allowing his magical bird companion to catch him and soar away majestically. Instead, he clung tightly to bird-Lotta's feathery neck and tried not to throw up as she leaped off her perch and launched into the sky. Nidhogg snorted and flexed his claws in frustration. The dragon blew out a sheet of flame, narrowly missing Lotta's feathery tail.

Lotta the swan spun in the air, trying to avoid the dragon's fiery breath, and she squawked as Whetstone gripped on tighter. The bird opened her wings and they sped downward, heading towards the ground in dizzying spirals.

The dragon shouldered its way past the few surviving branches and sprang out of the tree after them, its enormous leathery wings opening wide, hiding the tree from view.

Whetstone risked a glance behind them and immediately wished he hadn't. The dragon was following, blowing out bursts of fire. Lotta was forced to duck and weave to avoid being roasted mid-flight.

A large sign dangled from one of the branches ahead. Picked out in silver letters were the words: *Welcome to Midgard – please leave it as you found it.*

The ground raced up to meet them, brown and boggy with a scattering of familiar wooden buildings.

'YES!' Whetstone cried, the wind whipping through his hair. 'Over there, towards that boulder.'

Lotta flattened her wings, trying to slow down, but it was too little, too late. They hit the ground with a painful bump, tumbling head over heels through the bracken and wet grass. Whetstone rolled to a stop in a jumble of arms, legs and clothing. He lay breathless, tangled in a thorn bush. He checked carefully: all the bits seemed to be his, and he seemed to have all his bits.

He rolled away from the thorns and lay on his back, staring into the sky. The dragon circled above, twisting its long neck to glare around for them. It spat out a sticky fireball, setting alight a clump of long grass, apparently out of spite.

Lotta – no longer a bird – sat up and brushed ash off her clothes. 'We need to get out of here.' Her armour was singed, her dark face caked in soot along one side. A thin line of smoke wisped up from her curls.

Whetstone got to his hands and knees. Everything ached, even his eyebrows. He crawled towards the Valkyrie. Lotta patted herself on the head, putting out the last of the smouldering embers. Nidhogg looped overhead, his wings momentarily blocking out the sunlight.

'Are you all right?' Whetstone whispered.

Lotta wiped soot off her face. 'I'm fine. Just as long as Flee and Flay haven't been unfrozen and told Scold about us yet.'

Whetstone grinned. 'Nah, what sort of person would be crazy enough to do that?'

Chapter Eleven

Telling Tales

The stables of Valhalla were lit by a quivering green light. The magic holding Flee and Flay in place wavered but did not falter.

Thighbiter stamped his hooves in his stall. Despite being a flying horse, magic spells made him feel itchy. The air smelt wrong and his hooves prickled. He snorted and tossed his mane to try and frighten off the weird green light, but it made no difference. The weird green light stayed put.

Only Thighbiter was paying any attention as a shadow crossed the doorway and entered the stable. The horse whinnied.

'Shh.' The dark-haired boy laid a soothing hand on his side.

Leaving the horse, the boy circled the two girls. They were completely encased in the magical light, like insects stuck in amber. Faces frozen mid-scream, feet paused mid-step. He stopped next to Flee, peering into her startled face. But it wasn't the girl who interested Vali; it was the magic.

Carefully he reached out to touch the spell – the green

light was cold and hard. He laid his palm on it; it tingled like ice and smelt of mint. Vali pulled his fingers away and rubbed his hands together to warm them. He smiled – there was only one person in Asgard who could do magic like this: his Father.

Breathing deeply, Vali reached out both hands, placing his palms flat on the magic so the cold burned his skin. All he had to do was to find a flaw in the spell, and the whole lot would crack open.

Screwing up his face in concentration, Vali tried to focus on the feeling of magic under his hands. He might not have the powers that Loki did, but he had enough. Memories of his argument with his father kept forcing their way into his mind. Vali shook his head to try and clear it. No matter how hard he tried to concentrate, his thoughts burned through.

Just because he didn't get the cup, it didn't make him an idiot or a failure, despite what his father had said. Anger coursed through Vali's veins. His father had been going on about that stupid boy for years. Vali pushed all the hurt, and anger, and envy he felt into his hands. They glowed spookily against the green spell. A faint yellow light appeared around his pale fingers.

Vali pushed the feelings deeper into the spell. His father had said that Whetstone was important, all because of a stupid cup and a stupid riddle. But what if there was more to it than that? What if his father was planning to replace Vali with Whetstone?

Vali knew that Loki had been checking up on Whetstone over the years. He stashed him with that woman in Drott deliberately. The yellow glow intensified. A sharp line appeared between his hands. Vali gave a tight smile, his face deathly-white in the odd light. He had never cared about his father's plans for the cup and the harp; he just wanted Loki to stop spending all his time away from home.

With one last almighty effort, Vali felt the spell split apart. Shards of green ice flew across the stables, razor-sharp slivers striking the walls and roof. Thighbiter and the other horses whinnied and bucked in their stalls.

With a crash, Flee stumbled into Flay, grabbing her sister around the neck for support. 'Get it away from me!' She pointed at the spot where Whetstone had landed on the stable floor.

Flay squeaked in fear and tried to hide behind her sister. The two girls fell in a tangled heap.

Vali stepped forward, breathless from the effort of destroying the spell. 'It's all right – there's no one here but me.'

Flee pushed her long plaits out of her face. 'What?'

'Father trapped you in a spell. I freed you.'

Flee shoved her sister away and got up, peering about the empty stables.

Flay climbed to her feet, twisting what was left of her hair between her fingers. 'Hi, Vali.'

Flee looked at her sister, then back to the dark-haired boy. Deep shadows hung under his eyes, emphasizing his pale features. He looked miles away from his normally polished appearance. She put her hands on her hips. 'Well? Where's Loki and the boy?'

Vali paused, brushing the last magical splinters off his clothes. 'Who?'

'The boy. The – living – boy,' Flee huffed.

'A living boy?' A sour lump settled in Vali's stomach. 'What did he look like?'

Flay tossed her plait. 'Small, skinny, smelly. All the *S*'s.'

Vali's jaw tightened. *Whetstone*. 'Did Father say what he was going to do next?'

'What's the matter, Vali? Did Daddy not tell you what he was up to?'

Vali gave a painful smile. 'I know what he's up to. He thinks he can use the boy for something, but he's wrong. That boy is trouble.' Vali's fingers still burned cold from touching the magic. He ran his hand through his hair, leaving a trail of frost behind. 'So Father got you to bring Whetstone to Asgard?'

Flee tugged at her plaits. 'Ew, no. We brought back proper warriors from our battlefield trip. Lotta brought him.'

'Lotta?'

'You know, the rubbish trainee with the stupid dog. She was in the stables when we got here.'

'I knew he wasn't a real Hero,' Flay muttered.

Flee focused on Vali. 'Loki wanted our help to find the boy—'

'But instead he just appeared.' Vali rubbed his cheek. 'Lotta must have hidden him here.'

Flee put her hands on her hips. 'What's going on, Vali? Did Loki ditch us?'

'Looks like it.'

'But he promised to fix my hair!' wailed Flay.

Vali thought quickly. His father had never liked getting his hands dirty, so he'd probably sent Lotta and Whetstone to Midgard to get the cup. Vali smirked as an idea occurred to him. If Loki was using the Valkyries, why shouldn't Vali? They would be able to catch up with Lotta and Whetstone easily, and they might even be able to stop his father's endless trips to Midgard too . . . Odin wouldn't be pleased to hear that Loki had been meddling with humans again.

'So Whetstone arrived in Asgard by accident,' Vali mused aloud. 'Just think about how much trouble he could cause for the Valkyries if he gets caught.'

Flee and Flay exchanged a look. 'What does that mean?' Flee spluttered. 'Lotta's the one who's going to get in trouble.'

'Really? It's not going to look good for any of you. Just think – how is Odin going to react when he finds out his wonderful Valkyries brought a living human to Asgard?' Vali tutted. 'No one will ever respect the Valkyries again. This is about all of you now.'

'What do we do?' Flay whispered to Flee.

Vali pulled one of the ever-present knives out of his belt and twisted it between his fingers. 'You need to prove that it's all Lotta's fault. No one else's. You should tell Scold, right now. Then you can go after them, catch Lotta in the act of sneaking the living human back to Midgard.'

Flee narrowed her eyes.

'How long ago did Father freeze you? You'll have to move fast,' he added. 'They've already got a head start.'

Flee narrowed her eyes further until they were tiny slits in her face. Then she nodded. 'OK.' She nudged Flay with her elbow. 'Come on – let's go and tell Scold.'

'Start looking in Krud,' Vali called, spinning the knife in his hands. 'That's where she got him from.'

'Wait a minute,' said Flay. She turned back to Vali. 'What about your dad? He might be with them.'

The knife stilled in Vali's hand.

Flee stepped closer. 'Yeah, why is he so interested in Lotta's warrior?'

Flay nodded. 'The boy might not be a Hero, but he might be important for some other reason.'

Vali forced himself to smile. 'He's nobody. Father was wrong.'

Flay took a step closer and peered into Vali's face. 'There's something you're not telling us.'

With a flick of his wrist, Vali sent the knife spinning across the room – it stuck in a wooden post near Thighbiter's head. The horse bucked and reared in shock. Flay gasped in surprise. 'I said, he's nobody. Do you want to catch them or not?' he snapped.

Flee prowled towards the boy. 'If you're lying to us,' she said, giving him a poke. 'If this is some sort of trick . . .'

Vali held up his hands, a picture of innocence. 'Honestly, I just want you to catch them. Maybe you *should* mention Father's involvement. I'm sure Odin would like to know what he's up to.'

Flee gave him a hard look and a final poke in the chest. 'You're a loser, Vali. And just because you've helped us, it doesn't make us friends.'

Flay batted her eyelashes. 'Bye, Vali.'

'Leave him alone,' Flee muttered, pulling her sister out of the stable. 'That whole family is trouble.'

Vali lowered his arms as the girls vanished out of the door. He crossed the floor to retrieve his knife, smiling coldly as he imagined how the Valkyries would react when they found Whetstone. He stuck his knife back in his belt and left the stables to find his father.

Chapter Twelve

Ivor the Ankle Biter

Far below them, with his feet firmly back on Midgard's soil, Whetstone lurked in the shadows of a large boulder. 'I'm sure no one has even noticed you're missing,' he said to Lotta reassuringly.

The dragon soared overhead.

Lotta rubbed her elbow where a bruise was starting to appear on her dark skin. She climbed to her feet. 'So let's find the cup and get back before anyone does.'

The dragon twisted back down towards them. Shooting out a plume of fire, it set light to a nearby patch of brambles. Whetstone felt heat scorch the side of his face and he yanked Lotta into the shelter of the boulder. Nidhogg looped above, still searching for them.

'One problem. What are we going to do about *him*?'

'I'm sure he'll get bored and go back to Niflheim.'

Whetstone squinted at her. 'Really?'

'No, sorry.'

'We'll have to get rid of him before he sets fire to Krud. Maybe we could lure him away – he's chasing us, after all.'

'You want to fight a dragon? Careful – that sounds almost Heroic.'

Whetstone stuck his tongue out at her. 'Can you turn into a bird again? I'll make up another poem – a better one this time?'

Lotta shook her head. 'I'm not flying anywhere with that thing up there. Where are we, anyway? Is this Midgard?'

'You should recognize it – you've been here before.'

Lotta peered out from behind the boulder. 'Oh no, not . . .'

'Ivor the Nose Grinder,' they both said together.

Whetstone rubbed his hands together. 'But this is good news. See that big rock, the one with the runes that marks the edge of Ivor the Nose Grinder's farm?' He pointed at the branch of bracken sticking up in front of it. Lotta nodded. 'That's where I buried the cup.'

Lotta took a step forward. 'So let's get it.'

'No!' Whetstone pulled her back. 'The boulder is right out in the open. If we make a break for it, Nidhogg will definitely see us and use us for target practice.'

Lotta straightened her armour. 'But if we don't get the cup, Loki will tell everyone about what I did and I'll be banished.'

'You don't think he's going to keep his word, do you? Or if he does, he'll use it to blackmail you forever.'

Lotta wheeled around to face him. 'We're giving the cup to Loki,' she said woodenly. 'Are you still thinking about Fame and Fortune? Things have gone way beyond that now.'

Whetstone shrugged and glanced at the boulder again, trying to judge the distance. Every time he looked, the boulder seemed to be further away. 'We'll never make it. What we need,' he said slowly, 'is a diversion.'

Then, as if he had heard them, a tiny figure in full battle armour appeared next to the boulder.

Lotta stared. 'What is that?'

The figure beside the rock was dressed like a Viking but only about half as tall. The figure was roughly the same size across as it was up and down – it was like watching an angry beach ball waving a spear.

'Can't you read?! GERROFF MY LAND, YOU HORRIBLE REPTILE!'

'Ivor the Nose Grinder?' Whetstone and Lotta repeated.

'There's no way he could reach anyone's nose,' Lotta said in amazement. 'Ivor the Ankle Biter, maybe.'

'Or Ivor the Kneecap Crusher?'

Lotta bit her lip to hold in a laugh. The dragon had noticed the tiny Viking and was circling above in a tight spiral. 'What's he doing out there?'

'Dunno, maybe he thinks it's a minstrel.'

Lotta sniggered. She nudged Whetstone. 'But seriously, we're going to have to do something or he's going to end up as a scorch mark.'

'You're right.' Before he could think about it too much and change his mind, Whetstone stepped out from behind the stone. 'HEY!' He waved his arms. 'OVER HERE!'

'What are you doing?' Lotta grabbed his arm. 'You just stopped me from doing that!'

The dragon turned in mid-air, seeking out the source of the

new sound. Ivor took his chance and threw a spear. Nidhogg dodged easily and replied by gobbing a fiery spitball back. Ivor squealed and danced as the acidy dragon saliva stuck to his tunic and dripped off his horned helmet. To get rid of the stinging green spit, Ivor started pulling at his clothes, stripping down to his walrus-skin underpants before turning and running back towards his farm.

Having seen off the tiny Viking, the dragon turned to Whetstone and Lotta, a wicked gleam in his eye.

Whetstone dropped his arms, 'Uh-oh.' The dragon spun in the air and started to flap his way towards them.

Whetstone turned to Lotta. 'We're going to have to run for it.' She nodded. 'One . . .' Whetstone counted, rocking on his toes. 'Two . . . Thr—'

'THREE!' yelled Lotta, sprinting away from the stones. Whetstone hesitated, then took off after her, the edge of his cloak leaving a smoking trail in the air.

They plunged across the scrubby field, Whetstone expecting at any moment to feel his backbone turn to lava. Instead, the dragon flapped its great wings, creating a breeze that nearly knocked them over. Whetstone stumbled but managed to stay on his feet. The flapping wings threw hundreds of burning leaves and sticks into the air, pelting Whetstone and Lotta with dozens of red-hot pieces of shrapnel.

The boulder was getting closer. They were nearly there! As Nidhogg gave a roar of annoyance, Whetstone urged his legs into a greater burst of speed, the beating of Nidhogg's wings and the smell of burning sulphur close behind him.

Catching up with Lotta, Whetstone grabbed her arm and threw them both behind the boulder. Lotta fell at his feet, landing awkwardly as her ankle twisted beneath her. A jet of fire hit the stone, sparks cascading around the edges.

Lotta scrabbled for cover behind the boulder. She looked like she might be sick as she clutched her ankle. Whetstone was no doctor, but even he knew a foot facing the wrong way was bad news.

'Get the cup!' she yelled, giving him a shove.

Whetstone tore his eyes away from Lotta's twisted foot and threw aside the stick of marker bracken. He dropped to his hands and knees and dug frantically in the soil at the base of the boulder. Small stones scraped against his hands, and roots caught at his fingers. A metallic voice was just within earshot. It was the cup! A smile appeared on the boy's face.

'. . . left here like an old piece of rubbish – no one cares about me. I'm going to get all rusty . . .'

Whetstone burrowed deeper; his fingers brushed against cold metal.

'. . . serve you lot right if I never recite another poem. I've never been so under-appreciated . . .'

'Gotcha!' Whetstone pulled the cup free from the dirt.

The cup looked as annoyed as a cup can look – its rim had a distinct downturn, and the set of the handles made it look as though it had put its hands on its hips.

'Is that *it*?' Lotta peered over Whetstone's shoulder, her teeth gritted in pain.

The cup narrowed its ruby eyes. 'Oh. It's you.'

Whetstone rubbed some mud off the cup with his sleeve. 'I said I'd come back. I just couldn't wait to hear more of your fantastic poetry. But first we have to get out of here.'

'Whetstone, there's no way I can run anywhere,' Lotta said, grimacing. 'You should get out of here – take the cup and go.'

Whetstone's thoughts spun. 'No way. I'm not going without you. There's got to be something—'

Whetstone felt a thump, which travelled up through his feet and made his knees go wobbly. The dragon had landed in the field behind them.

'Well, don't ask me,' sighed the cup. 'I'm only a magical talking cup. I can't see *anyone* around here who might appreciate my poems.'

Lotta jabbed a finger at the cup. 'Of course – Nidhogg loves poetry! It's in the guidebook!'

'Fine poetry is well known for its calming effect on reptiles,' the cup continued. 'They know art when they hear it.'

Whetstone gritted his teeth, closed his eyes and stuck the arm holding the cup out from behind the boulder, hoping it wouldn't be bitten off.

Nidhogg took a deep breath, preparing a bolt of fire.

The cup began to speak:

> *I once had a hoard full of gold,*
> *And I thought, 'This'll never grow old.'*
> *I sat and I squished it,*
> *And then ate a biscuit,*
> *Then stood up cos my bottom was cold!*

Whetstone heard a funny rasping noise, like a sword blade being dragged repeatedly over a stone. He peered gingerly around the rock and took in the view, bit by bit. First the razor-sharp talons. Then the pointed tail flicking hypnotically in the air. The enormous body, red and gleaming in the sunlight. Gigantic leathery wings folded along its back. Enormous neck fins flexing in time with its breathing. Whetstone gulped. Nidhogg was very, *very* close.

'What's it doing?' Lotta hissed.

Whetstone peered up into the dragon's face. Yellow eyes glared down and steam poured out of its nose. But to Whetstone's surprise, the dragon's mouth was curved into an unmistakeable laugh.

He mouthed, '*It's working!*' at Lotta. She gave him a stunned thumbs-up.

'Another,' hissed the dragon through its long, pointed teeth.

Its breath hit Whetstone full in the face, stinking like a rubbish tip on a hot day. The dragon's own nostrils, each the size of Whetstone's arm, quivered.

'Go on.' Whetstone gave the cup a little shake.

A dragon's a terrible beast,

the cup began,

> *Who likes to eat gold in a feast.*
> *He burns it and bakes it,*
> *Then flips it and cakes it,*
> *He thinks it tastes good, at least!*

The scrapy sword noise came again. The dragon stalked back and forth in front of the boulder, watching the cup intently with large yellow eyes.

'More.' Clouds of steam blew out of his enormous nostrils.

> *I once knew a dragon called Mike,*
> *Whose bark was worse than his bite.*
> *He tried to breathe fire,*
> *But out came a wire,*
> *Which we used to fly a big kite!*

The dragon sniggered, his neck fins quivering.

Out of the corner of his mouth, Whetstone muttered, 'Try to put it to sleep.'

The cup twitched. 'Are you saying my poetry is boring?'

The dragon snorted, blowing a smoke ring.

Whetstone coughed it away. 'No, not at all. But you know what they say: a well-rested dragon is a happy dragon.' The cup considered this.

Nidhogg reared up on his back legs, his tail flicking impatiently.

Whetstone felt his knees go wobbly; he grabbed on to the boulder to keep himself upright. There he stood, weaponless and alone, in a field with nothing to stop him from becoming a lump of charcoal except a highly strung drinking vessel and a slightly rubbish Valkyrie with a busted ankle.

After what felt like an eternity of silence, the cup began to HUM. Whetstone tried to wave the cup in time with the humming. It sounded like a fingernail being scraped around the inside of a glass and made his ears vibrate unpleasantly. However, it seemed to be working on the dragon. The great yellow eyes began to sag and then close. The dragon was falling asleep.

In slow motion, Whetstone realized what would happen. With a great heaving snore, Nidhogg slumped forward, directly at the boulder protecting them.

'Move!' Lotta yelled, diving to one side as Nidhogg's body crashed towards them splattering mud in all directions.

Too late, Whetstone leaped the other way. The dragon's tail flicked round, catching his leg and tossing him high up into the air. Whetstone landed in a crumpled heap a few feet away, the cup still clutched tightly in his hand. Whetstone threw up his hands to protect his face as the tail came crashing down, landing across Whetstone's chest and pinning the boy underneath.

He felt the air being squeezed out of him as he lay trapped in the mud below the dragon's burning tail. He pushed and shoved at it – carefully at first, then with more urgency – as he tried to move it. Spines and sharp scales caught his fingers, nipping and drawing blood.

Lotta's pained voice came from somewhere behind the dragon. 'Whetstone?'

The cup squealed as Whetstone used it as an armoured glove to try and protect his fingers from the dragon's rough skin. But it was no use – Nidhogg wasn't going anywhere. And neither was he.

Chapter Thirteen

Dree Your Wyrd!

Lotta used the rock to lever herself up. Her ankle burned like fire, making her feel queasy. She swallowed and forced herself to focus. The heavy boot dragged on her twisted foot, but she dared not take it off.

Nidhogg snored, little gusts of smoke escaping from his nostrils. The smell made Lotta's throat feel thick. She gave up on standing, dropped to her knees and crawled towards the place where Whetstone lay trapped.

'Wotcha.' Whetstone waved at her with his free arm. His voice was cheerful, but his face was pale and strained.

'You're not getting stuck now.' Lotta stretched her arms around the dragon's enormous tail. It burned against her dark skin. 'We're taking that cup back to Asgard, if it's the last thing I do.' She heaved. A sheen of sweat broke out across her forehead and black spots flashed in front of her eyes. She pulled until her arms felt as if they were going to pop out of their sockets.

'I can't – it's too heavy.' She sank into the mud next to Whetstone's trapped body. 'It was a good idea though, putting the dragon to sleep. For a minute I actually thought it was going to work.' She smiled at him. 'You're not as thick as you look, are you?'

'Wow, Lotta – that was almost a compliment.'

'Don't get used to it.' She thumped him on the arm.

Whetstone smiled. It felt good to have someone on his side, even it was only because she needed him to get out of trouble with Loki. It was almost like having a friend.

Lotta rubbed her hands over her face. After a moment, she tossed her head back, soot drifting out of her dark curls. 'I guess it's all over. It's time to DREE OUR WYRD.'

Whetstone stopped smiling. 'What? Are you talking Epically again? Now? It really doesn't help.'

'*Dree your wyrd* means to feel sorry for yourself for what is about to happen to you. It's something Tragic Heroes do. Like when they're crushed by a dragon. Like you, right now. Maybe we could sing a sad song?'

'Please, don't.'

Whetstone gazed into the sky as he weighed up what to do. He was stuck under a dragon, but Lotta wasn't. She'd saved his life twice now – he owed her something, even if she was only helping him because she was scared of being banished. If she turned into a bird again, she might make it back to Asgard in time. She *had* warned him not to take the harp . . . Whetstone sighed. He always knew he wasn't cut out to be a Hero.

Whetstone made a decision. He picked up the golden cup, which felt cool and smooth in his hand. 'You should go, take the cup and get back to Loki.' With *almost* no hesitation, he tossed the cup towards her.

Lotta gazed at the cup but made no move to pick it up. 'What happened to Fame and Fortune?'

Whetstone shrugged, his shoulders squidging in the mud. Somehow Fame didn't seem so appealing any more.

'I can't just leave you here to be eaten by a dragon. It's not very brave or noble.'

'I'm not worth being brave or noble for. I'm a thief, remember?' Whetstone tried to grin, his face sticky with mud and sweat.

'I think you're worth a lot more than that,' Lotta muttered. 'For starters, you just tricked a dragon.'

Whetstone didn't know what to say. He turned his eyes upward. 'Somewhere up there is Asgard and Broken Tooth,' he reminded her.

Lotta groaned. 'This is all such a mess. I just want to go home.'

'So go. I'll be fine here on my own. And if I do end up in Snifflheim, at least I've already made a friend.' He patted Nidhogg's tail.

Lotta hunched her shoulders. 'It's Niflheim. And shut up, will you? I'm not going anywhere.'

Relief flooded through Whetstone. 'So you're not going to give the cup to Loki? You had me worried for a minute.'

Lotta snorted and threw a clump of mud at Whetstone. It missed, landing on the dragon's side, where it steamed. 'You were right. Even if he did keep his promise, he'd just hold it

148

over me forever. Maybe there *are* worse things than not being a Valkyrie.'

'Like being a human?'

'Like being in Loki's debt forever – it would be as bad as being Vali. Maybe I should just tell Scold and get it over with.'

'Are you sure? I don't think you're going to be able to convince her I'm a Hero. Heroes normally fight dragons, not get stuck under them.'

'Maybe there are different types of Hero,' Lotta mused.

'And different types of Valkyrie?'

Lotta shrugged. She wiped her hands on her skirt. 'So if you don't want the cup, and we're not going to give it to Loki, what are we going to do with it?'

Whetstone shrugged one shoulder. 'Give it back to Awfulrick, I guess. Except it doesn't belong to Awfulrick – it actually belongs to Frigg. I overheard Loki talking to those girls in the stables. They'd been helping him look for it.'

Lotta clenched her fists. 'And they wanted to get me into trouble!'

A low rumbling began. Lotta eyed Nidhogg. 'Someone's a heavy sleeper.'

'That's not Nidhogg.' Whetstone squinted up into the sky. 'It sounds a bit like . . . footsteps?' Something was moving in the clouds above them, coloured streaks coming together to form new shapes.

Lotta used the sleeping dragon to lever herself upright, her hand leaving a brief muddy imprint on the dragon's burning side. Her good foot landed on the cup and pressed it into the mud with a damp, sucking noise.

'It can't be,' she muttered, scanning the horizon. She unsheathed her sword and held it out in front of her, its point wavering in the air.

'What's going on?' Whetstone asked, watching as dots of rainbow light danced across the dragon's tail.

Lotta gulped. 'You should really read that guidebook some time. They've opened the Bifrost Bridge – it links Asgard and Midgard. Someone is coming.'

Whetstone held out his hand as the points of light sprinkled down on to his palm. It felt like icy rain. 'Who? No one but Loki knows we're here.'

The rainbow lights grew brighter, pouring down to form an enormous loop, trapping Whetstone and Lotta in the centre. Whetstone stretched out to touch the rainbow wall. It crackled and make the hair on his arms stand on end. The loop stretched and solidified, becoming a tunnel, which arched upward into the sky.

'I always wondered what was at the end of the rainbow.' Whetstone chuckled. 'It's me!'

Lotta stepped back, her bad ankle crumpling under her. She landed heavily on the ground, dropping her sword.

Whetstone peered up into the rainbow tunnel. A dark spot appeared. As it approached, it formed into the shape of a tall, armoured woman in a pointy helmet. Behind her lurked two girls with three long plaits between them.

'Oh no.'

Scold stamped to the end of the Bifrost Bridge, making

the lights quiver. She glared down at the boy and trainee Valkyrie. Her smooth olive skin had gone a dark, ominous red, her armour shining like the anger of the Gods. Scold sucked in an enormous breath, her massive chest swelling until she looked in danger of bursting out of her breastplate.

'BRINGS-A-LOT-OF-SCRAPES-AND-GRAZES!'

Lotta's eyes watered and her hair streamed out behind her.

'IN ALL MY YEARS OF BEING A VALKYRIE, I HAVE NEVER SEEN SUCH A BLATANT DISREGARD FOR THE VALKYRIE CODE!'

Lotta opened her mouth to speak, but no words would come out.

'NOT ONLY DID YOU BRING A LIVING HUMAN TO ASGARD – YOU THEN TRIED TO HIDE YOUR CRIME BY SMUGGLING HIM BACK DOWN TO MIDGARD AGAIN!'

Lotta stared at her grazed knees; she couldn't find the words to explain. Flee and Flay sneered down at her, their pale faces glowing with happiness.

'Do you mind speaking a bit more quietly?' called Whetstone. 'Only, you're going to wake the dragon.'

Scold squinted at him, her nostrils flaring like a pair of bellows. 'Never mind the *dragon* – right now we need to decide what to do with the CRIMINAL. Lotta, we were all stunned when you managed to get negative marks in axe-throwing, and your Epic Poetry is a disgrace, but this is a new low, even for you. I have never been more disappointed in a trainee.'

Lotta wrapped her arms around her knees, a ball of embarrassment.

'You are coming back to Asgard right now to explain yourself to Odin.' Scold clicked her fingers at Flee and Flay.

Lotta's head shot up. 'Wait – we can't just leave Whetstone here!'

The two girls hauled Lotta to her feet, her bad foot dragging uselessly, her sword left behind in the grass.

'That's exactly what we're going to do,' Scold sniffed.

'But he's stuck—'

'You are in enough trouble, young lady. Don't make it worse for yourself!'

The Bifrost Bridge contracted around the group of Valkyries. With a fizz of electricity, Whetstone felt the lights pass over his skin, leaving him outside the tunnel.

Whetstone shoved at the dragon's baking tail. 'Lotta! Come back!'

He could only watch as the rainbow light faded, taking Lotta and the Valkyries with it. The last thing he saw was Lotta staring at him, her face twisted in sorrow.

He lay back in the mud. *Who was I kidding? I'm not a Hero – I've let everyone down. Maybe I'm only good for sweeping out the wolf kennels after all.*

Whetstone rubbed his free hand over his eyes – the rainbow light had seared bright lines into his vision. A shadow fell across his face. Whetstone dropped his hand and squinted to try and see who, or what, it was. The figure took another step forward, and Whetstone's vision cleared.

He gasped in surprise. 'Light Finger?'

Chapter Fourteen

He'll Be Dead One Day

'CALL THE COUNCIL OF THE VALKYRIES!' Scold bellowed, unlocking the mighty gates of Asgard.

'Call the Council of the Valkyries!' Flee and Flay echoed, half carrying, half dragging Lotta towards the Valkyrie Training School.

'Let me go!' Lotta yanked her arms away from Flee and Flay, stumbling as they released her.

She hobbled slowly into the courtyard by the school where the Valkyries had assembled. They jostled into a semi-circular position, grouped together according to rank. The Class Ones in the middle, and Class Twos to the left. Lotta joined the Class Threes, huddling together on the right. All were turned to face the archway.

'All hail Odin, the Allfather, the Spear Shaker, the Terrifying One-Eyed Chief, the Leader of the Valkyries!' chanted the Valkyries as a tall, grizzled man with a blue cloak and one eye strode through the archway.

Behind him came a collection of glowing people. It wasn't often the Valkyries called a council, and no one wanted to miss out. Lotta recognized Thor, the God of Thunder, with his mighty hammer; beautiful dark-skinned Freyja, the Goddess of Love; and Odin's golden-haired wife Frigg, Goddess of Family. Even a few of the warriors from Valhalla appeared. Each of the warriors glowed faint blue, filling the courtyard with an unearthly light.

'Fight! Fight! Fight!' chanted one of the warriors. He stopped when he noticed Frigg glaring at him. 'Sorry,' he muttered.

Odin stopped in front of the Valkyries. In one hand he held a long wooden staff. Two ravens screeched and circled around him, bringing him news from across the Nine Worlds.

Flee poked Flay. 'Loki's not here.'

Flay craned her neck to peer around. 'Neither is Vali.'

'I knew he hadn't told us everything.'

'Oh dear, is your best buddy Loki missing?' Lotta hissed through gritted teeth.

Flee opened her mouth to reply.

A short Class One Valkyrie with tanned skin and lines tattooed across her fingers and face stepped forward. 'SILENCE!'

Flee's mouth closed with a snap.

'BRING OUT THE ACCUSED!' the tattooed Valkyrie commanded. This was Glinting-Fire, Odin's enforcer. She often stalked around Asgard carrying a clipboard, checking up on the trainees with on-the-spot quizzes. Lotta always failed. It wasn't that she didn't know the answers; there was just something about Glinting-Fire's dark, piercing gaze that always made Lotta's mind go blank. Once she even forgot her own name.

Lotta stepped into the centre of the courtyard. She dropped to her knees, pain shooting up her leg.

Odin peered down. 'Is this her?' he asked, his forehead creasing. 'She doesn't look like a criminal.'

Glinting-Fire snapped, 'Name?' Her thick plaits quivered on either side of her head.

'Um, Brings-A-Lot-Of-Scrapes-And-Grazes, Class Three Valkyrie,' Lotta stammered.

Glinting-Fire threw out her stubby arms. 'Bring forth the CODE OF THE VALKYRIES!'

Two Valkyries dragged a large stone tablet out of the shadows. It scraped unpleasantly across the bumpy ground, loomed over Lotta and cast her into shadow. She read the words carved into it:

CODE OF THE
VALKYRIES

1. BRING ONLY HEROES TO VALHALLA

2. NO WEAPONS IN VALHALLA

3. NO ANIMALS IN VALHALLA
(THIS MEANS YOU, BROKEN TOOTH)

4. BLADES MUST BE SHARP

5. SHIELDS MUST BE STRONG

6. BATHS MUST BE TAKEN AT
LEAST TWICE A YEAR

7. NO INTERFERING WITH MIDGARD

8. ANSWER ONLY TO ODIN
(AND BLOOD-RUNS-COLD)

'You are charged with breaking the Code of the Valkyries by bringing a non-Hero into Valhalla. How do you plead?' Glinting-Fire demanded.

Lotta swallowed, her words sticking in her throat. 'Technically I didn't bring him into Valhalla.'

Glinting-Fire's eyes blazed. 'But you do admit you brought a living human to Asgard?'

'I didn't mean to do it,' Lotta mumbled, staring at the ground.

'A confession of guilt! A terrible crime against the order of the Nine Worlds!' Glinting-Fire faced the crowd. 'It starts with humans, but where does it end? Who will she bring in next? Dwarves? Elves? GIANTS?'

Thor hefted his hammer thoughtfully. A warrior who appeared to be entirely made of scars and green tattoos tutted and shook his head.

Glinting-Fire turned to Odin. 'What is to be the punishment?'

Behind Glinting-Fire, Freyja rolled her eyes and stepped forwards. 'Shouldn't we hear what she has to say for herself first?'

Glinting-Fire glared at the Goddess of Love and Sorcery. 'There are *rules*, Freyja.'

Freyja dipped her head. 'Yes, and sometimes, Glinting-Fire, rules are broken for a good reason.' She turned to Lotta. 'Go on.'

Lotta lifted her head slowly. She glanced at the rest of the Valkyries, hoping for a friendly face. Akrid tossed her dreadlocks and sniffed. Flee and Flay were smirking. Lotta ignored them and focused on Odin's one remaining eye. 'It seems to me that the only reason I'm in trouble is because you don't think Whetstone is a Hero.'

'Who's Whetstone?' Odin asked.

'Must be the human she's been messing about with,' replied his wife, Frigg, patting him on the arm.

The Valkyries and ghostly warriors, most of whom looked like they had been put through a mincer and then stuck back together again, muttered to each other. Heroes were important. You couldn't have just anyone turning up and claiming to be one.

Odin tipped his head to one side, half of his face vanishing into shadow. 'Go on.'

'But if I can *prove* he's a real Hero, it would be OK that I brought him to Asgard. That's what Valkyries are supposed to do, isn't it? Bring Heroes to fill Valhalla ready for Ragnarok.'

At the word *Ragnarok*, the warriors cheered. A few waved their weapons – this is what they were here for, after all.

Flee piped up from the group of Class Threes. 'But he's still not dead – even if he is a Hero, which I doubt.'

'But that's just a matter of timing. I mean, he'll be dead one day, so maybe I'm just really, really early.'

'Pah,' snorted Flee.

The Valkyries and warriors muttered again. The man with the green tattoos murmured, 'She's got a point.'

Odin stroked his long white beard. 'That sounds reasonable,' he said at last. 'But he'll have to prove his worth beyond doubt.'

Lotta gazed up at Odin, hope flowering in her eyes.

'What is he going to have to do to prove it?' Glinting-Fire asked, tapping her clipboard. 'We need to set out the rules.'

The Gods and Valkyries all looked at each other for ideas.

'Beat up some Giants?' bellowed Thor, swinging his hammer.

Freyja tipped her beautiful head. 'Forge a magic ring?'

'Trust you to think of jewellery, Freyja.' Frigg tutted. 'How about capturing a sea monster?'

'Wait a minute,' said Scold, stepping forward. 'When we found Lotta, there was a dragon – Nidhogg, I think – on Midgard. Nidhogg shouldn't be on Midgard!'

'Perfect,' agreed Odin. 'Whetstone the human must send Nidhogg the dragon back to Niflheim.'

Lotta's heart sank. Whetstone couldn't even manage to get out from under the dragon. How in all of the Nine Worlds was he going to send it back to Niflheim?

A shriek came from the trainees, making everyone turn and look. Flay and Flee were laughing so hard they couldn't stand. Clutching on to each other, they fell on to the rutted ground.

'Defeat a dragon!' Flay chortled.

'He'll never manage that – not in a hundred years,' cried Flee, sitting up and wiping away tears of laughter with the corner of Freyja's skirt.

Freyja gave her a sour look and snatched her skirts away.

Scold ignored the giggling twins. 'But he'll have to do it alone.' She fixed Lotta with a hard look. 'No helping.'

Lotta struggled to her feet, trying to balance on her good leg. 'But shouldn't we at least tell him what he has to do?'

From the group of Class Twos, Akrid called out, 'If he's a real Hero, I'm sure he'll figure it out.'

Her freckled friend nodded. 'Dragons don't belong on Midgard – that much should be obvious.'

Glinting-Fire scribbled something on her clipboard. 'I'm fed up with second-rate Heroes making it to Valhalla. Someone needs to implement better standards.' She glared at Scold.

Frigg leaned forward; she patted Lotta on the head. 'They're only humans. Leave them to get on with it.'

Lotta winced as pain shot up from her ankle. 'He's not *only* a human. He's my . . . friend.'

Flay marched up to her. 'Get over it, Lotta – you failed. There's no way your loser "friend" will be able to get rid of the dragon, and you'll never be a real Valkyrie.'

'Yeah,' Flee agreed. 'Deal with it.'

Lotta smiled. 'I haven't failed, Flay. I'm just succeeding *differently*.'

Flay scowled.

Lotta grabbed on to Flee to help her balance. 'One question. How did you know about Whetstone anyway?'

Scold glared at them. 'Good point. And don't think I've forgotten about you two skiving off in the stables – it's still a mess in there.'

Flee shook Lotta off her arm. 'That wasn't our fault. He was late.'

Flay jabbed her in the ribs. 'Shh!'

'Who was late?'

Flee's eyes darted from side to side. 'Loki,' she said slowly.

A hiss escaped from between Freyja's perfect teeth.

'And Whetstone said that he'd heard them talking,' Lotta added quickly, limping towards Scold. 'They've been helping

161

Loki look for Frigg's magic cup!'

Scold exhaled through her nose, making her nostrils flare. 'WHAT HAVE I TOLD YOU ABOUT MESSING ABOUT WITH THAT MAN! You're supposed to be Valkyries – you serve Odin, not that selfish Fire Giant! Now get into Valhalla and start scrubbing tables before I get really angry!'

Without a backwards glance, the sisters scurried off into the enormous hall.

Thor tossed his hammer in the air and caught it by the handle. 'We should've guessed that Loki would be involved somehow.'

'Yes, let the humans deal with him this time,' Frigg agreed. 'I've had enough of his antics. Even if he finds my cup, it will be no use to him. I saw to that.' She pulled back her sleeves. 'To learn anything from the cup, Loki would have to find someone to speak to it for him. Someone whose fortune was closely linked to what Loki was trying to find out.'

Lotta gulped. 'Do you know what he's trying to find out?'

'I know *all* the fates of Gods and men,' Frigg preened.

'Loki is a Fire Giant,' Thor pointed out.

Frigg tossed her honey-coloured hair. 'OK, so that's a bit of a blind spot, but as long as he's out of Asgard, I couldn't care less.' Frigg spun on her heel and, taking Odin's arm, left the courtyard. Freyja gave Lotta an appraising look before following.

Scold clapped her hands. 'Right, girls. Back to Valhalla – we've got mead to serve.'

The trainee Valkyries groaned. The ghostly warriors

cheered and began to drift towards Valhalla.

Lotta's eye travelled to the handle of the iron key poking out of Scold's pocket. It looked very tempting. If she borrowed it for a bit, she could go down to Midgard, give Whetstone a helping hand and have him proved a Hero in no time. No one would ever know . . . Lotta grinned – she'd definitely been hanging out with Whetstone for too long if she was thinking about stealing things. Lotta limped closer to Scold, brushing her hand against her teacher's pocket.

Scold clapped a hand on to Lotta's shoulder. 'Not you.'

Lotta gulped, her fingers curling around the key. She turned to face Scold, pulling the key out of her pocket and tucking it beneath her wrist guard as she did so.

'I've got a special job for you. You're going to polish all the armour used by the warriors today. And when you're finished, you're going to polish it all again.'

Lotta groaned. She *hated* polishing armour.

'Go and get your ankle sorted out first, though. We can't have you limping about – it makes us look unprofessional.' Scold marched off towards Valhalla, chivvying the trainees along in front of her.

Lotta pulled the metal key out of her wrist guard. Behind her a raven cawed, watching her with glinting eyes.

Lotta put her fingers to her lips. 'Shhh.'

Chapter Fifteen

The Greatest Thief

Dragons are heavy, and this one was crushing the air out of Whetstone's lungs. The contrast between its warm skin and the damp mud was making Whetstone feel very peculiar. Hot, cold and breathless all at once, like he was getting a fever.

He stared up at the man standing over him.

'Light Finger?'

The man smiled, showing his ratty teeth. 'My, my, my,' he remarked, leaning on his staff.

'I never thought I would be so glad to see you!' Whetstone felt quite light-headed. 'You have to help me.'

Light Finger considered this, scratching his chin with a ragged fingernail. 'Yes, I could do that.'

'COULD!' Whetstone yelled, causing the dragon to twitch in his sleep. 'What do you mean, COULD?' He tried to drag air back into his chest. 'You HAVE to help me!'

'I don't HAVE to do anything,' Light Finger replied easily. 'What you fail to recognize here, Whetstone, is that I hold all the cards.'

'What cards? Who's playing cards? Just get this thing off

me! You don't understand – my friend's in trouble.'

Light Finger placed the end of his staff on Whetstone's shoulder and pressed down. 'I couldn't care less about your silly girlfriend.' He smirked as Whetstone sank. Whetstone started to protest, but Light Finger carried on. 'Valkyries who break their code deserve all they get. Now, I believe you promised me the cup.'

'How did you know she – was – a . . .'

Whetstone gazed up at the crooked man standing over him; the sun was cutting through the clouds, making his dandelion hair glow with red and gold lights. Whetstone screwed up his

eyes. With the thief's face half in shadow like that, he almost looked like . . .

'Loki.'

The man sneered and pulled himself upright out of Light Finger's habitual slouch. His face lost its rat-like appearance and gained some of the handsome looks Whetstone remembered from their meeting in Asgard. The scarred lips stretched into a broad smile. 'So you recognize me at last, boy.'

Whetstone's heart hammered in his chest; a prickle of sweat ran into his hairline. 'What are you doing dressed up as Light Finger?'

'I *am* Light Finger.' Loki shook his patched cloak over his shoulders. 'Or rather, Light Finger is me when I travel to Midgard.'

'But, why?'

'It's traditional. Gods always disguise themselves when they travel to the human world – have you never seen Odin in that ridiculous blue cloak and stupid hat he likes to wear?' Loki rolled his shoulders. 'Thanks for the ride down, by the way. Climbing Yggdrasil – it's a wonder no one had thought of it before.'

'You were that fat orange spider! You bit me!'

'It wasn't much fun for me either. Haven't you ever heard of soap?'

Whetstone's thoughts slowed. 'That was just before we found the harp.'

'I was trying to protect you. That harp was made by the Dwarves, and they don't like people touching their things.'

'Why put it in a tree then? Why not lock it up in a cave or a chest or—'

'Forget about the harp, Whetstone.' Loki waved the question away. 'You have far bigger problems at hand.'

Whetstone struggled against the dragon's tail. 'So you've been tricking me all along!'

'All your life, in fact. I wasn't kidding when I said you were going to be useful to me.'

'And you sent the Valkyries after Lotta,' Whetstone growled. 'You said we had a day before you'd unfreeze those girls.'

'No, that wasn't me,' Loki said thoughtfully. 'I had hoped we could get all of this sorted out without any extra attention. Awfulrick has been looking for you too. He has special plans for the boy who stole his magic cup.'

'Like what?'

'I'm not sure, but they were digging a big pit and sharpening a lot of wooden posts when I passed through Krud just now.'

Whetstone's skin went cold. 'What about Ivor's stables? You did something – knocked me out!'

'Wrong again, I'm afraid.' Loki smiled. 'That was Vali's idea. Jealousy is such an ugly emotion. He was worried that you were going to get all the Glory.'

'Death or Glory?'

'Indeed.' Loki leered at the boy. 'Think about the bigger picture here, Whetstone. Vali, Lotta, they're all in the past. You're here NOW trapped under Nidhogg – until he wakes up and wants some breakfast of course. If you want me to help you, then you have to help me. WHERE. IS. THE. CUP?'

'But I can't just forget about Lotta,' Whetstone cried. 'We have to help her!' The dragon's tail shuddered.

'The Valkyries have her now – she won't be coming back. She's probably scrubbing the floors of Valhalla in disgrace. If she's lucky.'

Whetstone tried desperately to wiggle his shoulders; the mud around the dragon was beginning to dry out and turn hard. If he didn't get out soon, he would be trapped – with or without the dragon.

'And I'd keep your voice down if I were you. Dragons are not good at mornings.'

A raven swooped past in the sky overhead as Whetstone's thoughts danced. He needed Loki to get him out from under the dragon, but he wasn't about to give up on Lotta – she hadn't abandoned him, after all.

Moving only his eyes, Whetstone glanced sideways to where the cup lay. It was covered in mud and half hidden under his sleeve, where Lotta had trodden it into the ground. Unbelievably, Loki hadn't spotted it yet.

'Are you sure you really want the cup?' Whetstone asked. 'It's so annoying. It never shuts up.'

The cup gasped. Whetstone pressed down on it with his elbow.

'The cup can tell you your fate,' Loki purred. 'Ask it one small, simple question for me, and you will have more Fortune and Glory than you have ever imagined.'

'Not Death?'

Loki shrugged. 'Maybe that too. It depends on the next five minutes. Then – if you value your own skin – you'll run far, far away. Awfulrick is not the most forgiving of Vikings.'

Whetstone nodded. The mud was setting hard – he really had to get out now. Loki wedged his staff over a rock and under the sleeping dragon's tail to create a lever. As he pushed down on the stick, inch by inch the tail lifted.

Whetstone wiggled backwards, out from under the dragon. He tried to pull the cup with him, but it was stuck fast in the rapidly drying mud. He knocked a clump of grass on top of it to hide it and heard a muffled 'Ouch!'

Whetstone clambered to his feet. He was sticky, dirty and brown from his shoulders to his ankles from lying in the mud. His chest felt like it had been hit with a sledgehammer. Whetstone gulped down big mouthfuls of air, feeling his lungs filling up.

Loki poked him with his staff. 'The cup?'

Whetstone rubbed his arm. 'This way.' He turned towards the collection of buildings on Ivor's farm.

Loki blocked his path with the staff. 'Vali searched that farm.'

Whetstone gulped. 'Obviously not hard enough. It's in the thatched roof of the stables.' Thinking of Ivor's warnings to travelling minstrels, he added, 'It'll be easy enough to find – if you start singing, it will join in.'

'You're lying.'

Whetstone opened his mouth to protest, but a voice reverberating down from above cut him off.

'VaaAAallLLlhallLLllla FoREveeeEEeer!!'

Twigs and feathers rained down around him. A whole bird's nest crashed to the ground. Whetstone threw his arms over his head and ducked out of the way.

With a terrible splatter, a large bedraggled bird plummeted into the mud behind the dragon.

Whetstone laughed in amazement. 'Lotta?' He scrambled towards her. 'You did it, and without any poetry this time!'

'Where are you going?' Loki growled, trying to trip Whetstone with his staff. 'You owe me the cup.'

Whetstone dodged the staff. 'I don't owe you anything!' He shot round the dragon's tail, skidding to a halt next to the trainee Valkyrie, now back in her human form and shaking feathers out of her black hair. 'What are you doing back here – I thought they took you to Asgard?'

Lotta winced, rubbing her ankle. 'Had to come back for my sword.'

Loki snarled, and stalked towards them. Whetstone wrapped Lotta's arm around his shoulders to pull her to her feet.

'I did a deal with Odin,' she explained, stumbling. 'We have to get rid of the dragon.'

'Oh, is that all? Easy-peasy. What about this guy?'

Loki lunged forward, flexing his fingers, green sparks arcing between them. Whetstone closed his eyes, waiting for the magic to strike. Beside him he felt Lotta tense. But before Loki could move, a mighty cry burst through the murk.

'GERROFF MY LAND!'

Chapter Sixteen

Family Un-Reunion

Whetstone dragged Lotta out of the way as Ivor the Nose Grinder marched towards the dragon, with Awfulrick and his band of Vikings looming threateningly behind him. 'I've had enough of this!' he yelled. He hadn't managed to scrape all the dragon dribble off his helmet, and several droplets clung to the horns, wobbling dangerously as he walked.

'You can all get off my land! Can't you read? Dragons! Cups! Minstrels! Weird bird-things that turn into people! You can all GET OUT!' He stomped up to the dragon and thumped it on the ear with his sword. The dragon woke up with a snort and peeled one eye open. Nidhogg obviously recognized the tiny Viking; he sniggered and blew out a delicate stream of fire to tickle Ivor on the backside.

'Argh!' Ivor clasped his burning bottom. He scuttled back towards Awfulrick and the rest of the Vikings, who had reached the edge of the field. Oresmiter pushed him into a patch of wet mud, splattering several nearby warriors.

Ivor sank gratefully in the mud as steam rose around him.

Whetstone swallowed, pulling his muddy hood up over his head; the last thing he needed was for Awfulrick to recognize him.

Dozens of Vikings in full battledress fanned out to surround the by now very angry dragon. A dragon who didn't like being woken up by a group of men in pointy helmets who were trying to poke him with swords.

'What in the Nine Worlds is going on?' Lotta panted, trying not to put any weight on her bad foot as they hobbled away from the Vikings and dragon. 'And where did Loki go?'

In a panic, Whetstone twisted his head about, searching for Loki's golden hair and patched cloak. But the man had disappeared.

In the distance, a rainbow twinkled. 'He must've used the Bifrost Bridge to go back to Asgard,' said Lotta.

'He wouldn't go – he hasn't got the cup yet.'

Taking his chance while Nidhogg was distracted with the arrival of the Vikings,

Whetstone helped Lotta hide behind a patch of brambles a short distance away. He dropped down next to her and lay on his stomach.

Whetstone carefully parted the brambles to peer through. A glint of gold poked out from the mud. 'The cup is still down there,' he said, pointing. 'In between the dragon's feet.'

Lotta swivelled round to lie down beside him. 'My sword is there too – Scold will go nuts if I lose it.'

'She's the least of your problems now.' Whetstone leaned on his elbow to look at her. 'What happened? You said you made a deal with Odin?'

Lotta pulled a twig out of her hair. 'You have to get rid of the dragon. That will prove you're a Hero – and if you're a Hero, I haven't broken any rules.'

'I'm not dead though.'

'You haven't survived this yet.' Lotta grinned.

'What about Loki – could he still have you banished?'

'Odin is in charge of the Valkyries, not Loki. He can't banish me without Odin's say-so, and now Odin knows the truth, he can't manipulate me any more. I just need to turn you into a Hero, and I'm done.'

In front of them, the dragon spat fire and beat his wings, accidentally knocking over a group of Vikings who had been sneaking up on it from behind. A prickle of sweat broke out between Whetstone's shoulder blades. A second group narrowly avoided being set on fire as Nidhogg turned to see what was happening near his tail. Whetstone swallowed. 'Get rid of the dragon, yeah. Any idea how?'

'C'mon, it can't be that bad. You already got out from under his tail.'

'That was Light Finger – I mean Loki. Loki is Light Finger. He helped me, but it was all a trick – he's been planning this my whole life.'

Lotta leaned up on her elbow. 'He needs you to talk to the cup for him. Frigg told me that's the only way he can find out what he wants to know.'

'But *what* does he want to know?'

Lotta poked him on the forehead. 'Think! It must be something he knows is in your future.'

'There's nothing in my future.' Whetstone huffed. 'I'm no one, just an orphan from Drott who grew up with a wolf-obsessed crazy lady.'

'Not just an orphan – you were found. It must have something to do with what happened to your parents!'

Whetstone felt like a hole had opened up inside his stomach.

Awfulrick's voice boomed over the field, 'SO WHAT WE'RE GOING TO DO IS – ATTACK IT ONE AT A TIME!'

Whetstone and Lotta peered back through the brambles as the Vikings gave a loud cheer and stampeded away from Nidhogg.

'IT'S MORE SPORTING THIS WAY,' the Viking Chief continued. 'AFTER ALL, THERE IS ONLY ONE DRAGON!' The Viking horde cheered again and started lining up one behind the other, the ones at the back taking the opportunity to wipe down their helmets and sharpen their weapons.

Whetstone shook his head, trying to clear away the swell of unfamiliar emotions. He swallowed. 'They're going to get killed. They should have just left it alone. It was asleep.'

A man with tufty pigtails charged at the dragon, his sword held high. 'ArArArArGHHHH!'

Whetstone and Lotta winced as Nidhogg swiped forward with his front foot, sending the man flying across the field. A cloud of arrows filled the sky from the Viking line; Nidhogg incinerated them with a single burst of flame. Ash rained down on the pair hiding under the bush.

Lotta sat up suddenly. 'What is he doing here?'

The back of his neck prickled, and with a sinking feeling Whetstone realized Lotta wasn't watching the Vikings, she was looking at something over his shoulder. He twisted around. 'Vali!'

Vali's face looked even more sickly now – he seemed hollow. His arm shot out and grabbed Whetstone's elbow, dragging the boy to his feet.

'Let *go*.' Whetstone yanked at Vali's hand – it was freezing cold, like a fistful of icicles.

'I suppose you think you're better than me,' Vali spat. A trickle of sweat ran down the side of his white face. 'But you're not. Your pathetic quest is going to fail.' The boy squeezed Whetstone's arm painfully.

Lotta scrambled to her knees. 'What are you even doing here? You should be in Asgard.'

Vali glared at her. 'You'd like that, wouldn't you? Keep me out of the way.' He dragged Whetstone closer.

Lotta lunged sideways to avoid being skewered as a smoking spear thudded into the ground next to Vali's foot.

Whetstone tried to pull the older boy away. 'We have to move. We're going to get killed!'

A knife appeared in Vali's free hand. 'No, just you.' He slashed forward, his eyes cold with hatred. Whetstone dodged sideways trying to avoid the blade, but Vali tightened his grip on Whetstone's cloak, dragging him back. 'Father was wrong – there's nothing special about you. He wasted all those years watching you when he could have . . . spent them with Mum and me.'

Whetstone choked as the fabric tightened around his throat. Stars flashed in front of his eyes as he dropped to his knees. He could just make out Lotta's face as she started to crawl towards him, her brown eyes wide.

Vali hissed into his ear. 'Say goodbye, Whetstone. This is the last Valkyrie you're ever going to see.'

Darkness crept into the edges of Whetstone's vision. Flashes of memories appeared before his eyes: the Angry Bogey's wolf kennels; the lights glinting off Awfulrick's magic cup; the glowing people in Asgard . . .

Then the pressure around his throat lifted as his cloak was released. Whetstone sprawled on to the ground, wheezing. He heard Lotta gasp.

Light-headed, Whetstone turned to look behind him. Vali lay on the ground. Standing over Vali, holding his staff in both hands, was Loki.

Whetstone gazed from one face to another, stunned. Up close, Vali looked worse than ever, his face almost waxy, but then his eyes fluttered open.

'Surprised to see me, Father? I had to use the Bifrost Bridge to get here, so it took me a while to catch up.'

Loki snorted. 'Couldn't stay away, could you? You've already made a mess of searching for the cup. I've just been to look through that stinking farm myself.'

Vali clambered to his feet, rubbing his head. Loki and Vali eyed each other with cold, burning hatred.

Lotta reached out and grabbed Whetstone's sleeve, muttering, 'Let's get out of here.'

He nodded, forcing himself to concentrate. He looked around, searching for Awfulrick. The last thing he wanted to do was run away from Loki and into Awfulrick.

The Vikings had stopped for a breather. They were sitting on the grass and heather in small huddles, tending to their burns and scorches with a pale yellow ointment.

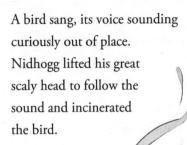

A bird sang, its voice sounding curiously out of place. Nidhogg lifted his great scaly head to follow the sound and incinerated the bird.

As smoking feathers drifted across the field, Nidhogg took another great breath and surrounded himself with a wall of fire.

Whetstone scrambled to his feet, pulling Lotta up beside him. She leaned heavily on his arm, using him as a crutch.

'It's over,' Vali spat at Loki. 'I released the two Valkyries you trapped . . .'

Lotta growled low in her throat.

'. . . I've had enough of you vanishing and leaving me and Mum – it's humiliating. Everyone knows about you and Angrboda.' With a bang and a flash of green light, Vali flew backwards, landing on his back a few paces away.

Whetstone's head snapped round, all thoughts of leaving forgotten. 'The Angry Bogey?' he rasped, the words burning in his throat.

Vali lifted himself on his elbow. 'He's not special – you

should've left him to die, not taken him to that woman!'

'You took me to the Angry Bogey – I mean Angrboda?' Whetstone corrected himself at Loki's expression.

'Oh yes, he's been looking after *you*!' Vali spat.

'So this *is* something to do with my parents!'

Vali laughed, a sickly sort of noise.

Loki fixed his eyes on Vali. 'I needed Angrboda to keep an eye on him for me, until he was old enough to be any use. We knew he would be the key to finding the rest of the Skera Harp.'

'Wait – the Skera Harp?' Lotta asked. 'That harp we saw in the tree?'

'Oh dear, Father. Your top-secret hiding place isn't so top secret after all.' Vali smirked, rolling on to his back and staring up at the sky.

'What does the harp have to do with my parents?' Whetstone gulped. 'They weren't minstrels, were they?'

'The harp, your parents, they're all tangled up together. And Father thinks you –' Vali pointed at Whetstone – 'are the only one to untangle it.'

Whetstone fought to keep his face blank as hope surged in his chest. His parents were connected with the harp, and he had found the harp, so maybe he could find them too? Then a vision of the harp tumbling down Yggdrasil flashed though his mind and his hopes fell with it.

Lotta hobbled forward. 'But if the harp is so important, why have you been trying to get the cup all this time?'

'The harp's not complete,' Vali answered, still staring

upward. 'It's useless without the strings.'

Lotta tipped her head. 'So the cup knows where the strings are? But why do you think it will tell Whetstone? We never even saw the harp before today.'

'Because the strings aren't the only things that are missing,' Loki replied. He turned to the boy. 'Are they, Whetstone?'

Whetstone looked up.

'*Once upon a time*,' Vali began in a sing-song voice, '*two Dwarves built a magical harp.*'

'You need to stop talking.' Loki aimed a kick at his son. Vali rolled away.

'*The frame was made from the wood of Yggdrasil itself,*' Vali recited. '*The strings were said to come from impossible things: the footfalls of a cat, the roots of a mountain and—*'

'Since you seem determined to tell them,' Loki interrupted, 'we should start from the beginning.'

Loki grabbed Whetstone by the back of his tunic, dragging him off his feet. Producing a cloud of sparks with his free hand, Loki cast them into the air. A dark tunnel opened where they fell. Loki stepped into the tunnel, pulling a stunned Whetstone after him, and Lotta, snatching Whetstone's hand at the last moment, was yanked into the tunnel with them.

❀

The world changed. Gone was the field outside Krud, Vali, and even the dragon. Instead, Whetstone found himself in a

181

dark and dripping cave. Lotta banged into his shoulder.

'What's she doing here?' Loki snarled.

Lotta brushed down her armour. 'I hitched a lift.' She tested her ankle carefully. 'Ha! You fixed my foot!'

Whetstone stared at the cave in shock. 'Is this where my parents are?'

'Be quiet!' Loki rubbed his temples. 'You're in my memories.'

Lotta wrinkled her nose. 'Yuck.'

'Welcome to the world of the Dwarves.' Loki glared at Lotta. 'We're deep in the caves of Svartalfheim.' He turned to Whetstone. 'You're privileged – the first human ever to see this.' He pushed Whetstone forward. 'Go on.'

Ahead of him the corridor twisted and turned. With no other options, Whetstone crept forward, the low ceiling scraping his head, his eyes struggling to see in the dim light, Lotta's boots bumping into his heels.

A clanging reached his ears. Eventually a red light appeared, spilling into the corridor and making the damp walls shimmer. The scent of sulphur burned Whetstone's nose, reminding him unpleasantly of the dragon.

'Twelve years ago, I heard that the Dwarves were working on something new,' Loki's voice echoed behind them. 'A harp with extraordinary magical powers.'

Whetstone stepped through an arch; the ceiling rose and a large cavern opened up in front of him. His breath came more easily.

Loki stopped in the archway. 'So I decided to come and see the harp for myself.'

The sound of metal striking metal echoed, making Whetstone's ears ring. Through clouds of steam and showers of red sparks, Whetstone could just make out a low structure. A forge.

'Don't worry,' Loki called. 'They can't see us. It's not real.'

Whetstone ran his hand over a nearby boulder. Strands of something green stuck to his fingers. He wiped his hand on his trousers – it felt real enough.

A bright light cut through the smoke, burning Whetstone's eyes. The light faded, revealing two short, dark-skinned men, both with enormous beards and pointed ears. One held out an enormous pair of tongs to his companion, who pulled on a thick pair of leather gloves and plucked something from the end of the tongs. The two men bent their heads together to examine the object. They spoke in a rasping language Whetstone didn't recognize. One of the Dwarves held the object up; it was a silver string, glowing in the dim light.

'A harp string,' Lotta breathed.

As she spoke, the Dwarf with the gloves turned to the workbench behind him, on which stood a magnificent wooden harp. The same harp they had found in Yggdrasil, but unbroken. Two silver strings were already fastened to its polished body. The Dwarf fumbled in his thick gloves to attach the third.

'When played separately, each of the strings has a different power. When played together, they are more powerful still,' Loki explained.

Whetstone crossed his arms. 'I still don't see what this has to do with me or my parents.'

'You will. Now, watch. This is the good bit.'

A large black horsefly flew low over Whetstone's head, making him duck. It entered the room, buzzing around the two Dwarves, distracting them. The Dwarf holding the tongs swiped forward, trying to swat the fly, muttering all the time in his rasping language. Loki laughed from his position in the doorway, as instead of hitting the fly, the Dwarf smacked his companion in the face with the tongs, knocking him into the workbench. The harp slid along the surface of the bench, before crashing to the floor.

With a flash of green light, the fly transformed into the tall, handsome form of Loki. He scooped up the harp with a cold laugh.

'But why?' Lotta asked. 'You can do magic already – why bother with the harp?'

'That harp has a very particular gift,' the man began. He

was interrupted as, with a roar, the Dwarves realized what Loki was up to. They made a grab for him and the harp, barrelling all three of them to the floor. There was a sickening crunch as the wooden frame split apart.. The man fought his way free and, with a tumble of feathers, he transformed into a falcon, which leaped into the air, clutching the silver strings and broken shards of wood in his claws. Loki the falcon shot over the Dwarves' heads and out into the dim tunnels, the Dwarves chasing after him.

Whetstone looked at the real Loki. 'Where did you go?'

Loki smiled. He opened his hand. Green light shone from the sparks in his palm, casting strange shadows on to his face. He poured the sparks into the air. The Dwarves' cave vanished. Whetstone stumbled into Lotta as a wide sandy beach appeared around them. A forest of dark pines crept in behind.

'Midgard.'

Whetstone's pulse thudded loudly in his ears. He looked around, desperate to take it all in. A smallish wooden house stood off to one side. A woman sang from inside the house, words that were both familiar and strange. Whetstone staggered forward, Lotta following.

'Is that your home? It's . . . nice,' she offered.

In front of them a man strained to pull in a fishing net. He paused, bending forward to extract a feathery tangle from the net. A large bird and several shining strings flashed in his hands. Whetstone headed towards him, his feet feeling like they were dragging through treacle. Every crunch of the sand echoed loudly in his ears, the scent of pine stinging his nose.

'I took a wrong turn when I left Svartalfheim.' Loki grimaced. 'I should have made it all the way back up to Asgard. Travelling between the worlds is hard enough when you're human – it's even more difficult when you're a bird.'

Lotta snorted.

The fisherman carefully untangled the falcon and laid it down on the beach. He held up the strings, which blazed in the sunlight.

Whetstone had almost reached the man; the world seemed to slow down. He tried to breathe around the hard lump in his chest. He reached out a hand to touch him on the shoulder. 'Dad?'

The world around them froze and turned grey. Whetstone took another step and found himself falling. He landed face first back in the mud of Krud. With an '*Oof*!' Lotta landed beside him. The sound of the dragon beating his wings filled the air.

Vali was lying where they had left him. He pushed himself up. 'What did you show them?'

Whetstone scrambled up. 'That was my dad – take me back!'

Loki grabbed Whetstone's arm to steady him, but the boy yanked himself away, rounding on Loki. 'It was you! You broke up my family. I could've had a normal mum and dad instead of that . . . that . . .' His fingers opened and closed in frustration.

Loki edged closer. 'There are things you have to understand about the harp, Whetstone.'

Blood fizzed in Whetstone's veins – he had been so close to his home, his family. He shrugged off Loki's arm. 'I don't care about the stupid harp, just bring my parents back!'

Lotta got to her feet. 'Tell us, what happened after Whetstone's dad found the strings?'

'The Dwarves knew Father had taken the harp and they wanted to stop him from using it,' Vali explained. 'So after he stole it, they cursed it.'

Loki aimed another kick at his son, catching him on the knee. Vali fell back, groaning. Loki turned back to Whetstone with a smile. 'Vali is right – the Dwarves put a curse on the harp, but it didn't take hold immediately. I woke up on the beach and went to your parents' hut to get the strings back.'

Whetstone glared at the Trickster, forcing himself to pay attention to Loki's words. Anger, hope and sorrow for all that he had missed swirled together, making his chest feel tight. He didn't know whether he wanted to cry or to kick something. 'What did you do to them?'

'I didn't do anything. I watched as your father gave your mother one of the harp strings . . . She looked so pleased,' he said, his face a picture of sympathy. 'I can't imagine she was used to such finery, judging by the state of their cottage.'

Whetstone glowered, his fingernails digging into his palms.

'But then she started fading away. She was gone – who knows where. Your father didn't last much longer – another of the strings was still sitting on his palm as he vanished. You were left with the third, tied round your wrist like a bracelet.'

'Where did they go?' Lotta asked. 'And why was Whetstone left behind?'

'That is a question only the cup can answer,' Loki replied.

'So that's what you're up to!' Lotta pointed her finger at Loki. 'Frigg told me her cup wouldn't speak to you. She said you would have to find someone whose fate was linked to ask it questions instead. That's Whetstone, isn't it? You need him to speak to the cup for you. You think that his fate is to find his parents – and where his parents are, the strings are too!'

Loki gave a pained smile. 'What a clever little Valkyrie.'

'But why has it taken you so long to find them?' Lotta asked. 'Midgard isn't that big.'

'Because they're not on Midgard,' Vali called. The others wheeled around to face him. Vali looked sicker than ever; he clutched his knee. 'The Dwarves didn't know where Father had taken the harp, so they decided to separate the strings, making the harp useless. The strings were sent to three different worlds, and as Whetstone's parents were holding them, they went too. We know one of the worlds was Midgard because he –' Vali waggled a finger at Whetstone – 'stayed behind. But his parents could be in Asgard, Vanaheim, Alfheim, Svartalfheim – maybe not Svartalfheim . . . They could be anywhere. Anywhere but here.'

Whetstone's eyes opened wide in shock. Then his brow creased. 'That's . . . impossible.'

Lotta looked at him sideways. 'That's why you're all by yourself,' she said quietly. Whetstone remembered her fear that she would be exiled to Midgard, cursed and alone. He tried to smile reassuringly at her.

Loki reached out and squeezed Whetstone's shoulder. 'I felt guilty about what happened to your parents . . .'

Vali snorted a laugh.

'. . . so I've been keeping an eye on you over the years.' Loki smiled sympathetically. 'It was never my intention for your parents to get involved. They were just in the wrong place at the wrong time. But now you can help me get them back.'

The boy stared at his feet for a moment, trying to steady his thoughts. 'But that's not what you said earlier. You wanted me to ask the cup a question, then to run away.' He looked up at Loki. 'You don't want to help me to find them – you just want the harp.'

Loki smiled, his scars twisting his lips into strange shapes. 'You really are very clever, Whetstone. It was all a test to make sure you were up to it. It's not going to be an easy task, tracking them down, but Angrboda assured me you were ready.'

Whetstone closed his eyes at the memory of his life with the Angry Bogey. He forced himself to take a deep breath. He clenched his fists to stop his hands from shaking. 'You gave me to her.'

Loki stepped towards Whetstone. 'I saved your life. You were only a baby. Without me, you would have died alone in that fisherman's hut.'

'And *because* of you, I lost my parents.'

'And *with* me, you can get them back.'

Whetstone took a few steps away. He had gone so long without parents that he had almost forgotten that they must have existed, but deep down, he'd always hoped there was someone out there looking for him, wondering if he was OK. New emotions surged in his chest, making his heart thump painfully. Maybe this was the answer, and Loki was right. If his parents really were trapped in different worlds, it might be possible to get them back. He glanced at Lotta, who was watching him with wide brown eyes. Travelling between worlds sounded impossible, but he had already visited Asgard today . . . 'All right – how?'

Lotta sucked in a breath.

'All we have to do is repair the harp.'

Whetstone's head spun. They had dropped the harp down Yggdrasil and it had probably been burned to a crisp by now.

'I have repaired the wooden frame – that's what you found in the tree. We just need the strings.'

Lotta tossed her dark head. 'Yeah, the harp in the tree. Well, we – sort of – knocked it down. It's probably in Niflheim now. That's what woke up –' she jabbed a thumb over her shoulder – 'him.'

Loki crossed his arms. 'I know. That's why I bit you – to try and stop you from touching it.'

'He was the spider,' Whetstone explained to Lotta's raised eyebrows. Behind them Vali began to laugh.

Loki ignored him. 'It would take more than Nidhogg to destroy the harp frame – it's made from Yggdrasil's wood. We just have to go to Niflheim to retrieve it.'

'So you broke it when you took if from the Dwarves, but it will survive Niflheim? You're nuts, Loki,' Lotta scoffed.

'Dragon fire won't harm it, otherwise Yggdrasil would've burned long ago.'

Despite Lotta's doubts, hope bubbled in Whetstone's chest.

Vali dusted himself off. 'Of course, Father hasn't told you what the harp does.'

Loki spun towards his son, snarling.

'Listen to me – you can't help him.' Vali's eyes were fixed on Whetstone. 'Played together, the strings have the power to cut holes in the walls between the Nine Worlds. That's what its name means – *Skera*, "to cut". I think the Dwarves were jealous. They wanted to impress Odin, to prove that they could travel between the worlds, just like the Gods can.'

Lotta gasped. 'Open the walls? Are you mad?'

'Get away from the boy, Vali,' Loki snapped. '*He's* going to help me now.'

'Father's going to use you, just like he used me.' Vali grabbed Whetstone's arm, his fingers digging in like claws. 'I thought if I helped him, he would see what he's been missing. That all this chasing after the harp wasn't worth it. He's been looking for the strings for twelve years. He tried the Norns, the runes, even the Well of Mimir, but nothing could tell him where the strings were.' He peered into Whetstone's stunned face. 'Don't give him the riddle, Whetstone. Your parents are probably dead by now – living humans won't last long against a Giant or a dragon.'

'What are you saying, boy?' Loki roared.

Abruptly Vali released Whetstone and wheeled around to

face his father. 'The truth! You don't want to help him find his parents and fix this. You just want the power the harp can give you.'

Loki faltered in shock at the anger in his son's voice. Awfulrick and the Vikings turned to see what the commotion was, a few of them standing up to get a better look.

Vali threw open his arms. 'Just imagine what it would be like with nothing to separate the worlds. Frost Giants finally invading Asgard. Dwarves ravaging the Elves' gold mines. Dragons burning everything on Midgard.' He pointed a finger. 'And Father in charge of it all.'

Whetstone went cold.

'Why can't you see what you already have: me, and Mum and our home?' A trickle of spit flew out of Vali's mouth. 'Why isn't that enough? You keep chasing after power, but what difference would it actually make?' Loki turned his head away, and Vali limped a few steps forward, closing the gap between them. 'Just – stop.'

Loki half turned back towards his son and raised one hand. For a moment Whetstone thought he was going to say something to comfort Vali, but instead a crackle of green light shot towards the boy, knocking him sideways.

Vali stumbled, then stopped, his feet suddenly too heavy to move. He stared down as his legs began to turn grey and cold. He struggled to raise a foot but couldn't. Vali looked up, his face frozen in shock as his legs, then body, hardened like a statue.

'He's turning to – stone?' Whetstone spluttered as Vali lost the use of his arms. Loki glowered at his son, his eyes glittering.

Lotta put her hands over her mouth, streaking mud on to her face.

Vali managed to raise his head, the skin on his neck and face darkening and becoming solid. He opened his mouth to speak. 'I—'

Daylight flickered, like something passing in front of the sun. In the place where Vali had once stood, there was a boy-sized boulder, nothing more.

Lotta stared wide-eyed at the place where Vali had been. Behind her, one of the Vikings let out a low whistle and shook his head. Whetstone felt Lotta's fingers slide into his palm.

Loki turned back to the boy. 'The cup has the riddle. It knows where your parents are, but thanks to Frigg's magic, it will only tell *you*,' he purred. 'Think about it, Whetstone. Don't you want to find out what happened to them? With my help, you can put your family back together.'

Whetstone hesitated, his eyes darting from side to side. More and more Vikings were approaching now, drawn by the spectacle of Loki's magic. He and Lotta were gradually being surrounded by a heavily armoured circle.

Loki peered into the boy's face. 'All I want in exchange are the harp strings. I'd be doing you a favour really. It's the strings that are keeping you apart. Let me deal with them, and you can all be together again.'

Lotta squeezed his hand. 'You don't have to do this by yourself,' she murmured. 'We'll get the cup together.'

Whetstone squeezed Lotta's fingers in return, then glared at the handsome man with the twisted lips. 'I wouldn't trust you with a teaspoon, let alone a magic harp that could fill Midgard with monsters. I'd rather fight a dragon than help you.'

Loki's expression turned sour.

'I don't need to fix the harp to find my parents; I just need the cup. I don't want to be part of your schemes, no matter how much Fortune and Glory you promise. I wouldn't get it anyway – look at what you just did to Vali.'

'WHERE IS THE CUP?' Green sparks flashed between Loki's fingers.

Whetstone swallowed. Lotta shifted beside him. They couldn't give in, no matter what Loki did. He *had* to get the cup and get rid of the dragon. Whetstone braced himself for Loki's attack.

Even the surrounding Vikings seemed to hold their breath, their armour clinking gently in the silence as everyone waited to see what would happen.

'OI!' a voice called out. The Vikings turned as Awfulrick strode past Loki, his eyes fixed on Nidhogg. He pointed a sausagey finger at a golden object poking out of the mud in between the dragon's feet. 'THAT'S MY CUP!'

All heads swung in the direction of the dragon, who puffed out his neck fins at the attention.

Awfulrick spun back around, small dark eyes glinting in his red face. 'BY ODIN'S TOENAILS, THAT'S THE THIEF!' he bellowed, pointing at Whetstone. 'ORESMITER! GRAB HIM AND DON'T LET HIM GET AWAY!'

Chapter Seventeen

Plenty of Dragon to Go Around

Whetstone felt his feet leave the ground as Oresmiter the Puffin Eater picked him up by the collar of his shirt. His boots dangling helplessly, Whetstone's heart thudded loudly in his ears; he had escaped Loki, only to be caught by Awfulrick.

'What happened to you?' Oresmiter chuckled. 'You're all muddy.'

'I'm sorry I took the cup, but I can get it back,' Whetstone panted, trying not to be strangled by his own cloak, his throat burning again.

'Put him down!' demanded Lotta, marching over to Awfulrick and smacking him on the arm. 'We've got stuff to do!'

The enormous man turned his piggy eyes on her. 'GRAB THE GIRL TOO – SHE COULD BE HIS ACCOMPLICE!'

Lotta shrieked as she was thrown over Oresmiter's shoulder, her boots kicking at the air.

Awfulrick glared at Whetstone. 'WE'LL DEAL WITH YOU BOTH AFTER WE'VE FINISHED WITH THE DRAGON!'

Whetstone's ears rang – he thought he might be going a bit deaf from being so close to Awfulrick. 'I'm going get rid of the dragon too,' he bargained. 'Just give me a chance.'

The Viking Chief screwed up his face in thought. Whetstone crossed his fingers, hoping that he wouldn't pick the pit of big spikes.

'ALL RIGHT,' Awfulrick said at last. Whetstone went limp with relief. 'BRAGI, GIVE HIM YOUR SWORD AND SHIELD.'

Oresmiter dropped Whetstone to the ground as a tall youth with red hair and a highly polished helmet stepped forward. Whetstone groaned. He remembered Bragi, the boy who had sneered at him over the eyeball stew, which – he realized with a jolt – had only been last night. Lotta pushed herself up on her arms, trying to see what was happening over Oresmiter's shoulder.

Bragi did not look impressed to be giving his weapons and shield to Whetstone. He stuck out his lower lip before dumping them on the ground with a clang.

'DON'T WORRY!' cried Awfulrick. 'YOU'LL GET THEM BACK WHEN THE THIEF HAS BEEN BURNED TO ASHES!'

Bragi smirked at this thought, but then glared at Whetstone. 'It's not fair – he's just a kid. It was my turn. I want to have a go at the dragon.'

'YOU WILL, MY BOY!' bellowed Awfulrick, slapping him hard on the back. 'THERE'S PLENTY OF DRAGON TO GO AROUND!'

'Are you sure about this?' Ivor the Nose Grinder called from somewhere at the back. 'It could be some sort of minstrel's trick!'

'SHUT UP, IVOR. HE DOESN'T LOOK VERY MUSICAL TO ME!'

Loki reappeared at Whetstone's side. Under the guise of pulling the boy to his feet, he muttered, 'It's not too late – just say you'll help me get the cup, and I can get you out of this. Remember, the cup can tell you where your parents are.'

An image of Vali hardening to stone flashed across Whetstone's mind. 'You mean it can tell me where the harp strings are?'

Oresmiter gave Whetstone a shove. 'Get on with it,' he grumbled, ignoring Lotta as she pounded on his back with her fists.

Whetstone straightened his shoulders and examined the weapons. The sword was bigger than he was, with a dark green scabbard. He wiped his clammy hands on his trousers and tried to pick it up but could barely lift the handle.

Bragi crossed his arms, his muscles bulging against his gold armband.

Whetstone gave up on the sword and picked up the circular shield. 'I'll just have this,' he said to Awfulrick, who laughed.

'THAT'S THE SPIRIT, GIVE THE BEAST A CHANCE.' Awfulrick's beard twitched into a grin as he took off his own iron helmet and dropped it on to Whetstone's head. Whetstone staggered, then pushed it back a bit so he could see. Loki reappeared behind Awfulrick, his expression unreadable.

'OFF YOU GO!' Awfulrick shoved Whetstone towards the dragon. The other Vikings started to beat their swords on their shields, *thump*, *thump*, *THUMP*, in encouragement.

❀

Nidhogg lay on the ground in a large patch of scorched earth. He watched the Vikings with interest, wondering what they were going to do next. Idly he picked at a scale with his claws. He had quite enjoyed knocking the warriors over and blowing fireballs at them. It made a nice change from trampling the spirits of the unworthy dead back in Niflheim. These Vikings had a lot more life in them.

So Nidhogg was surprised when a boy crept towards him clutching a too-large shield. He didn't even have a sword. Nidhogg flexed his neck fins and waited. The cup lay between his rear feet, forgotten in the grass.

❀

Lotta pushed herself up on her arms, Oresmiter's shoulder was digging into her stomach uncomfortably. Twisting on her side, she could just see Whetstone as he slowly approached the dragon. He held the shield up as high as he could, the weight of it making his arms shake. Lotta gasped as the dragon blew out a plume of fire, Whetstone ducked down behind the shield just in time. The air suddenly filled with the smell of burning hair.

Whetstone rubbed soot out of his eyes and peered behind him, catching Lotta's eye. She tried to grin in an encouraging way as Scold's words echoed in her head: *He'll have to do it alone, no helping.*

Lotta bit her lip and watched as Nidhogg drew in a deep breath. Whetstone lifted the shield, waiting for the flames. But instead the dragon lazily blew a smoke ring, which drifted across the field, wrapping itself around the boy. It was letting him approach. This did not feel like a good thing.

'Stop messing about,' Lotta muttered. 'If you get eaten, I'll never make it back to Asgard.'

A flash of movement behind the dragon caught Lotta's attention. A rabbit hopped out from behind a boulder and bounced towards the dragon. In a flash of golden fur, the rabbit changed into a stoat that zipped along the length of Nidhogg's tail, and the stoat then turned into a frog, which

leaped in between the dragon's feet.

Lotta twisted around, trying to see if Loki was still with the Vikings. An empty space stood next to Awfulrick. She tried to call out a warning, but her voice was lost in the thumping from the Viking shields.

Whetstone had seen the shapeshifter too. He lowered the shield, staring. The frog was now a green-and-orange butterfly, landing on one of the dragon's hind claws as it flapped its wings.

'Loki?' Whetstone's voice sounded tiny from across the field.

Lotta gritted her teeth. Scold had told her not to help him get rid of the dragon, but no one had said *anything* about helping him stop Loki. Lotta reached down and stuck her hands into Oresmiter's armpits. 'Tickle, tickle, tickle!'

With a shriek, Oresmiter tossed the girl into the air. Lotta landed on the ground with a thump. She rolled away from Oresmiter, snatching up Bragi's sword and swinging it over her shoulder in one movement. Dodging away from the rest of the Vikings, Lotta began to march across the field to join Whetstone.

Whetstone's eyes were fixed on the butterfly. With a dull green glow, the insect twisted and grew, moving through various forms until it settled in the shape of a man.

'What are you doing?' he called to Loki. 'Get out of there!' Nidhogg blew out a jet of fire and Whetstone quickly hoisted up the shield, the metal burning his fingers where the flames heated it.

Loki gave him a cold smile. 'I've waited for long enough. I'm going to get those harp strings, with or without you, boy.' The man was just behind Nidhogg now, using its bulk to block what he was doing from Awfulrick and the other Vikings.

'You can't get the riddle without me,' Whetstone called.

'Is that right?' Loki's form blurred and shrank into a duplicate of Whetstone. 'Cups aren't too clever,' the man said in Whetstone's voice. 'I'll find another way of getting the cup to give me the riddle, and when I have the riddle, maybe I'll find what's left of your parents too.'

Whetstone's knuckles went white as he gripped the shield.

'Don't listen to him,' Lotta called out. Out of the corner of his eye, Whetstone could see her hauling the heavy sword across the dried mud behind him

'When I repair the harp, I'll be able to control the balance of the Nine Worlds.' Loki-Whetstone's arm snaked around the dragon's leg, fingers fumbling for the cup half buried in the mud. 'Odin will be nothing compared to me!'

Whetstone edged a couple of steps closer, his eyes fixed on the glint of gold. A few more moments and Loki would have the cup, and through it, the key to opening the walls between the worlds. If Loki got his way, it would mean the end of everything – all the monsters from the stories would be able to reach Midgard. One dragon was bad enough; Whetstone didn't want to imagine a world full of them.

'Whetstone!' Lotta yelled. He looked up to see Nidhogg's tail aiming straight for him.

Throwing Bragi's sword aside, Lotta charged forward, grabbing Whetstone around the waist in a flying tackle. They rolled head over heels through bracken and heather.

'Thanks,' Whetstone panted, disentangling himself.

'Why are there two of you?' Lotta asked, pulling twigs out of her black curls. 'It's creepy.'

'That one's Loki. I'm just glad you can tell us apart.'

'It's easy, that one is better looking.'

The dragon hissed a laugh, its tail whipping around for another go.

'Use the cup again,' Lotta yelled, throwing her arms over her head.

'That's it!' Whetstone spun towards the dragon. 'Oi, cup!' he yelled as loud as he could. 'Your poems are rubbish!'

The cup, which had been silent for longer than it ever had been before in its entire existence, suddenly started shrieking and throwing itself about. Then several things happened at once.

One: Nidhogg looked down in surprise at the cup at his feet.

Two: There was a yell as Awfulrick and the other Vikings spotted a second Whetstone lurking behind the dragon.

Three: Loki-Whetstone scooped up the cup in triumph and it screamed in his hands, flashing white hot.

Four: Loki transformed back into his usual self. He took a step backwards, smoke pouring from his blistering hands as he fought to keep hold of the burning cup.

Five: Unfortunately this meant that Loki was standing on the dragon's tail. Nidhogg couldn't really feel the shapeshifter, as he was tiny compared to the house-sized dragon, but that was not the point. Dragons have a very strong sense of personal space, and Loki was far too close.

Six: Nidhogg roared in anger, flashing his crimson wings. He leaned down, and . . .

Seven: Swallowed Loki, and the cup, down in one almighty gulp.

Lotta crawled to where Whetstone was crouched behind the shield with his eyes tight shut, waiting for the crunching and chewing noises to stop.

'There's no way the cup will be answering questions now,' she muttered.

A hard lump formed in Whetstone's chest; he'd lost the chance to find his parents. Behind them, the Vikings fell silent.

Lotta peered round the shield. 'Is it over?'

Nidhogg reared up on his hind legs, towering over the boy and girl. He burped.

'I'm sorry, Lotta – I tried, but I'm not a Hero,' Whetstone said, as the ball of damp fire rolled towards them. 'All we're going to be now is a burn mark on the heather.' But instead of incinerating them, the soggy fireball dispersed as it passed over them, leaving only a lingering smell of warm toenails.

The dragon opened his mouth.

'RRRRRRAAAAAAGGGGGGHHHHH!' A belch of sulphuric breath sprayed over the field. Hiding behind the shield, Lotta choked and spluttered as Whetstone wiped at his streaming nose. Something gold glinted inside the dragon's mouth.

The dragon roared again – this time it sounded like it was in pain. Whetstone felt Lotta get to her knees beside him. She squeezed his shoulder as Nidhogg opened his jaws. 'It's in his mouth!'

'What is?'

'The cup! It must be hurting him and distracting him from finishing us off.'

Whetstone peered into the dragon's dark mouth. Wedged between two of the dagger-like teeth was the cup. Nidhogg picked at it with a claw, and the cup gave a metallic squeal.

Nidhogg shook his head, trying to knock the cup free. Whetstone and Lotta ducked as acidy drool flew everywhere.

Lotta turned to Whetstone. 'This is your chance! You just need to pull the cup out of its mouth.'

Whetstone wiped his stinging eyes. 'You cannot be serious!'

Lotta nodded. 'It's perfect. Nidhogg will owe you a favour and after he's gone you can ask the cup for the riddle.'

Whetstone gulped. The dragon squinted at them with gleaming yellow eyes.

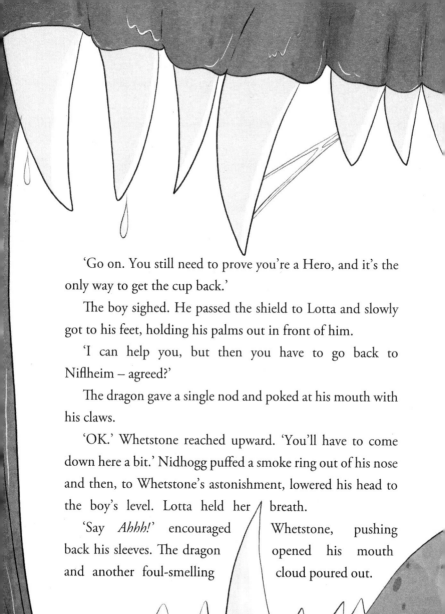

'Go on. You still need to prove you're a Hero, and it's the only way to get the cup back.'

The boy sighed. He passed the shield to Lotta and slowly got to his feet, holding his palms out in front of him.

'I can help you, but then you have to go back to Niflheim – agreed?'

The dragon gave a single nod and poked at his mouth with his claws.

'OK.' Whetstone reached upward. 'You'll have to come down here a bit.' Nidhogg puffed a smoke ring out of his nose and then, to Whetstone's astonishment, lowered his head to the boy's level. Lotta held her breath.

'Say *Ahhh!*' encouraged Whetstone, pushing back his sleeves. The dragon opened his mouth and another foul-smelling cloud poured out.

Whetstone closed his eyes and pictured his parents in their cottage by the river. He thought of Lotta arriving back in Asgard and being covered in slobber by Broken Tooth. He told himself that this was the only way to make these dreams into reality.

Holding his breath, he carefully stretched one hand into the dragon's mouth, waiting for jaws to snap closed over it. He slid his hand in further and further, until his whole arm was inside Nidhogg's dark mouth, and at last he felt his fingertips brush against the cup. He carefully looped his fingers through one of the handles before giving it an almighty tug. The cup popped free, sending

Whetstone tumbling backwards into a thorn bush.

Nidhogg sat up, probing his teeth with his gigantic tongue. Clearly feeling much better, the dragon smirked at Whetstone, raising one scaly eyebrow. Whetstone grinned back, relief flooding through him.

The dragon shot a fireball into the air. He *was* feeling better. He had had a great day, full of chasing, fighting, poetry, and now he had eaten a large meal and didn't have anything pointy stuck in his teeth any more. It had been fun, but what he wanted now was a nice snooze on his bed of bones and broken armour back in Niflheim.

The dragon rose slowly into the air, the draft from its wings making helmets fly across the field and knocking Ivor the Nose Grinder sideways into a patch of nettles. Majestically Nidhogg flew up and up towards the clouds, the Vikings below giving appreciative '*Oohs*' and '*Aahs*'. In a final farewell, Nidhogg looped-the-loop and dived low over the Vikings before swooping high into the sky and off into the distance.

Lotta tossed the shield aside and punched Whetstone on the arm. 'I *knew* you could do it – you are a Hero!' She dragged her sword out of the mud and slid it back into the scabbard strapped across her back.

Whetstone pulled himself painfully out of the thorn bush. The cup was covered in sticky green slime.

'That was disgusting,' the cup complained.

'Agreed.' Pride welled up in his chest – he'd done it! Defeated the dragon, got the cup and stopped Loki. He wiped the cup with his sleeve. 'I just need to ask you something,' he began, but was stopped by a thumping noise from behind him.

Whetstone turned to see the crowd of Vikings cheering and banging on their shields in triumph. Awfulrick led the charge, and they stormed towards him and Lotta.

'WELL DONE!' Awfulrick pulled Whetstone into a bone-crushing hug, and the air was forced out of his lungs for the second time that day. Whetstone tried not to sneeze as the bearskin waistcoat tickled his nose.

'YOU SHOWED THAT DRAGON WHO WAS BOSS, HUH?!' bellowed the Viking Chief, releasing Whetstone and slapping him on the back. Whetstone wheezed and felt his ribs pop back into place.

Awfulrick snatched the streaky cup out of Whetstone's hand. 'THERE YOU ARE, YOU LITTLE BLIGHTER!' He gave the cup a squeeze.

'Whoops!' the cup giggled.

Whetstone straightened his tunic. 'I'm sorry for taking it. I know it was wrong . . .' He glanced at Lotta, who rolled her eyes. 'But I was wondering if I could just borrow it for five minutes? There's something I need to ask it.'

Awfulrick popped the cup on to his shoulder – it sat there like an annoying metallic parrot. He slapped Whetstone on the back again. 'ANYONE WHO CAN STICK THEIR HAND INSIDE A DRAGON'S MOUTH AND WALK AWAY IS FINE BY ME!' Awfulrick turned to the rest of the Vikings. 'BACK TO THE VILLAGE! WE'LL HAVE MINSTRELS MAKE UP SONGS ABOUT *THIS* BEFORE NIGHTFALL!'

The Vikings cheered in delight. Oresmiter threw his helmet up into the air, where it turned a passing raven into a cloud of feathers.

The Vikings swarmed around Whetstone, hoisting him up on to their shoulders. The Viking choir launched into a song:

> *Asgard! Asgard!*
> *Home of Gods and fun.*
> *Asgard! Asgard!*
> *Until the Frost Giants come.*

Lotta yanked on Awfulrick's arm. 'Wait!'

Awfulrick patted her on the head. 'DON'T WORRY – YOU CAN COME TOO.'

> *Valhalla! Valhalla!*
> *The place where Heroes go.*
> *Valhalla! Valhalla!*
> *When they're slain by their foe!*

'You have to STOP!' Lotta shrieked. She pointed into the sky.

'What is it now?' Whetstone yelled back as the Vikings bounced him high into the air. 'It's over.'

Lotta shook her head. 'Not yet.'

Whetstone managed to twist around in the air to see what Lotta was pointing at.

The air was filled with the sound of thundering hooves – it sounded like a whole herd of horses galloping towards them.

Whetstone screwed up his eyes, expecting to see the Valkyries returning, but instead in a flash of gold a single horse and rider appeared. A horse with . . . eight legs.

Whetstone gulped. 'Is that . . . ?'

Lotta nodded, transfixed by the sight.

Awfulrick and the Vikings came to a shuddering halt, watching the golden horse approach. It landed softly on the earth in front of them, sunlight gleaming off its shining coat. It pawed its many legs, churning up the half-baked mud. A tall man in a blue cloak slid down from the saddle, his wide-brimmed hat casting his expression in shadow. He lifted his head to reveal a grizzled face and one missing eye.

Mutters and gasps came from all around as the Vikings realized who he was. The man produced a staff, driving it solidly into the ground. Two large ravens landed on the perch on top, one of them giving Oresmiter a dirty look.

All around Whetstone, Vikings started dropping to their knees. He felt Lotta grab his sleeve and pull him down to kneel beside her on the ground.

'Hear me,' the one-eyed man intoned. 'For I am Odin, the Allfather, the Spear Shaker, Chief of the Gods.'

Chapter Eighteen

The Cup Speaks

The air felt flat and still. Full of static, like a storm was on the way. Whetstone tilted his head sideways; everyone else had gone very quiet.

'Lotta?' he hissed.

A raven croaked loudly. Whetstone glanced up. Watching him intently was Odin.

'They cannot see or hear us, nor will they remember what happens in this time,' the God explained.

Whetstone stood up. Slowly Lotta got to her feet beside him. 'What do I do?' he muttered.

Lotta shrugged. 'Something brave? He's come to decide if you're a Hero.'

'I am a Hero.' Whetstone grinned. 'I got rid of the dragon, didn't I?'

'With my help!'

'I didn't see *you* volunteering to put your hand inside his mouth!'

'Ahem.'

They both looked up from their whispered conversation.

Lotta's fingers twisted together nervously. 'So, we were wondering if Whetstone has proven he's a proper Hero? Am I allowed to go back to Asgard?'

Odin's beard twitched into a smile. 'I'll have to have a word with Scold about raising your Collecting Fallen Warriors score.'

'Yes!' Lotta fist-pumped the air. 'I knew it!'

The Allfather jiggled his staff. One of the ravens took flight, sweeping low over the frozen Vikings before using his claws to snatch the golden cup from Awfulrick's shoulder. The bird dropped it at Whetstone's feet.

'Men have fought and died for that cup. Do you know why?'

Whetstone nudged it with his toe. 'Loki said it had powers – it could tell you your fate.'

Odin sighed; one of the ravens ruffled his feathers. 'It once belonged to my wife, Frigg, and like her it knows all the fates of men and Gods. But unlike Frigg, it will actually tell you,' he finished, under his breath.

Lotta nudged Whetstone with her elbow. 'Tell him about Loki.'

Whetstone looked up. 'Loki wanted the cup to tell him a riddle – well, tell *me* a riddle to repeat to him. There was this harp, made by the Dwarves—'

'Frigg gave the cup a very specific skill,' Odin interrupted. 'It can tell the future, but only of the person who holds it. It wouldn't tell Loki what he wanted to know directly. He had a . . . *falling-out* with Frigg, and now he can't even hold it in his hands. Frigg thinks that will be enough to stop him, but I'm not so sure.'

'So Loki was right.' Lotta gestured to Whetstone. 'Whetstone's fate *is* to find his parents – and the missing harp strings.'

Odin sighed. 'Fate is a complicated thing. You can have more than one, depending on the decisions you make. Your fate could be to return the harp to the Dwarves, or it could be simply to have scrambled eggs for tea.'

Whetstone glanced up, determined. 'Not me. I know I'm going to find my parents and bring them back to Midgard.'

Odin's beard twitched into a smile. 'Would you like to be sure?'

Whetstone stooped to pick up the cup; it felt cold and glassy under his fingers as he turned it over in his hands. His family might have been destroyed by Loki and the Skera Harp, but it didn't have to stay that way. Whetstone realized that Odin was right – his fate depended on the choices he made now, and whatever the cup said, he was getting his family back.

He held the cup up to his mouth. 'Go on then, tell me my fate.'

In a thin but clear voice, the cup replied:

> *You will seek to find, those who have been pulled apart.*
> *A journey high and deep, into Yggdrasil's heart.*
> *One you will find below, in an ice-locked land,*
> *Still living but alone, for Hel holds him in her hand.*

The other you will find, bound by a glittering chain.
She is kept for her tears, they fall as golden rain.
The pieces must all be sought, and joined once more as one,
None shall be whole until Loki's crime is undone.

The cup's voice faded away, echoes bouncing around the frozen Vikings.

Whetstone dropped the cup on to the ground, the words ringing in his head. He had no idea what they meant, but it was a start!

Lotta's face scrunched up. 'What was all that about?'

'I'm sure you're not expecting me to answer that,' Odin replied. Whetstone looked into the God's face. It was said he had exchanged one eye for knowledge and that his ravens flew endlessly around the Nine Worlds bringing him news. Whetstone wondered how much he already knew. 'I will tell you one thing: Loki won't stop looking – for you or the harp strings.'

'But Nidhogg ate him!' Whetstone spluttered.

Odin smiled. 'You don't know Loki if you think that will finish him. Whetstone, you may not have intended to find yourself in the middle of Loki's schemes, but you are perfectly placed to be the one who stops him. It is not yet the time for Ragnarok. The Nine Worlds must remain separate. It would be *Heroic* indeed if the harp strings were found and returned to the Dwarves before Loki gets his hands on them.'

Whetstone gulped. 'I'm not sure I'm the right sort of Hero to—'

Set in his tanned face, Odin's eye twinkled brightly. 'Maybe it's time for a new sort of Hero . . . and a new sort of Valkyrie,' he added, turning to Lotta, who puffed her chest out with pride.

'But if you know what Loki is up to, why didn't you stop him?' Whetstone asked.

'I am stopping him. I have placed you in his path,' Odin replied. 'It will be interesting to see what his next move is.'

Whetstone goggled. 'Me against Loki?'

Lotta smiled. 'I almost feel sorry for Loki.'

Whetstone straightened his shoulders. 'So . . . it's save the harp strings, save my parents, save the Nine Worlds?'

Lotta laughed. 'You're getting the hang of being a Hero after all!'

Sleipnir whinnied, shaking his golden mane. Odin climbed back into the saddle. 'Good luck, Whetstone. I will keep an eye out for you, but it is time for us to return to Asgard.'

'I guess this is goodbye, then, thief boy!' Lotta thumped him on the arm again. 'I kind of wish I could come with you. Valkyries usually only get to see Heroes after they're dead. It's been fun seeing what you get up to beforehand.'

'Fun, yeah. If by fun you mean nearly getting burnt, eaten, falling to our doom, or banished.'

Lotta grinned. 'The important word there is *nearly*.'

Whetstone reached in his pocket for the crumpled guidebook to the Nine Worlds. He held it out to her. 'Don't forget this.'

Lotta tossed her head. 'I think you'd better keep it – you

can give it to me next time I see you,' she added with a wink.

Odin reached down to pull Lotta up behind him.

'Say hi to Broken Tooth for me!' Whetstone called as Sleipnir bunched up his muscles and leaped into the sky, showering Whetstone with mud and dust. Lotta waved as they shrank into the distance and vanished into the clouds.

Chapter Nineteen

You Were Wrong – He's Not Dead

Whetstone groaned but kept his eyes shut. He wasn't sure where he was, and once people knew he was awake, things he wasn't prepared for might start happening. He stretched out his fingers and felt the ground beneath him. Grass and leaves: he was outside.

Whetstone peeled one eye open. The sky over him was darkening – how long had he been asleep? Twisting his head to the side, he found himself gazing at a pair of thick, hairy ankles.

'UP YOU GET!' Awfulrick shouted cheerfully, hoisting Whetstone to his feet by the neck of his tunic. 'YOU'RE THE LAST ONE TO WAKE UP. OI, ORESMITER! YOU WERE WRONG – HE'S NOT DEAD!'

Whetstone rubbed his eyes. 'What happened?' The events of the last day were starting to catch up with him: a disturbing swirl of dragons, gigantic trees, flying horses and bad poetry.

Awfulrick shrugged. 'WHO KNOWS THE WAY OF THE GODS? EXCEPT YOU, OF COURSE!' He slapped Whetstone so hard on the back it made the boy stumble forward.

Whetstone shuddered as a memory surfaced. 'I didn't really stick my arm inside a DRAGON'S MOUTH, did I?'

Awfulrick laughed and wandered off towards some other large, hairy men. Whetstone spotted Oresmiter wiping a mountain of bird poo off his helmet. He smiled to himself, remembering the ravens.

Seeing the cup lying innocently in the long grass, Whetstone scooped it up, intending to hand it back to Awfulrick. It seemed impossible that he had stolen it only yesterday, thinking it would bring him Fame and Fortune. Whetstone ran his thumb over the ornate metalwork and smiled. It had brought him something better: a clue to help him find his parents. Oh, and a crazy quest against Loki for the enchanted harp strings.

'Did that all really happen?'

The cup gazed up at him with its ruby eyes, then it opened its mouth and began to speak:

> *There once was a young lad from Drott,*
> *Who everyone thought was a clot.*
> *He got rid of a dragon,*
> *Will he fall off the wagon,*
> *And go back to thieving or not?*

'No, definitely not. Good to see you're back to normal, anyway.'

The cup blew a loud raspberry.

'Come on, everyone – back to Krud! We have a victory feast to eat!' called Oresmiter, who had given up trying to chip off the bird poo.

'Songs to sing?' added Ivor the Nose Grinder, waving his bogey-encrusted helmet in the air. Oresmiter nodded.

'And . . . poetry to recite?' asked Whetstone, handing the cup back to Awfulrick.

❀

A few days later, Whetstone was sitting by himself in the Great Hall of Krud. Most of the villagers were clustered up at the far end of the hall listening to Awfulrick's cup recite more rude poetry.

> *There once was a lad named Whetstone,*
> *Who everyone thought was a moan.*
> *He started off zero,*
> *But turned out a Hero,*
> *But I still wouldn't give him a loan!*

'Well, I guess that's almost as good as singing songs about me,' Whetstone muttered.

A few of the other Vikings gave him sidelong looks and whispered to each other. Stories of his adventures had been spreading. Awfulrick had invited him to stay in the village, and it seemed as good a place as any while he tried to figure out the riddle.

One you will find below, in an ice-locked land,
Still living but alone, for Hel holds him in her hand . . .

An old woman slopped a bowl of something indescribable down in front of him, cutting into his thoughts. He glanced at it, felt his stomach roll and pushed it away.

Whetstone got to his feet and headed out of the door into the bright sunshine. He felt in his pocket for the guidebook Lotta had given him:

Helheim: *Home of the Queen of the Dead, Hel.*
Yes, she named the place after herself. Tells you
everything you need to know, really.

Except it didn't. Whetstone didn't know how to get there or what to expect from the Queen of the Dead. But Odin had set him the task of stopping Loki, and if that meant he had to travel to Helheim, he knew he had to try. Just because he didn't have big muscles and cheese for brains, it didn't mean he couldn't be a Hero.

Tipping his head backwards, Whetstone enjoyed the feeling of sun on his face as something flashed past, making him flinch in surprise. An arrow thudded into the grass by his feet. It was heavy and black, and it was on fire.

Tied to the arrow was a piece of paper. Taking care not to burn his fingers, Whetstone untied the smoking parchment and flattened it out carefully. It was a letter from Lotta. Whetstone was glad Lotta had made it back to Asgard, although it felt odd not to have her stomping around any more.

With a grin, Whetstone began to read . . .

WHETSTONE THE BOLD
CARE OF CHIEF AWFULRICK
VILLAGE OF KRUD
NEAR SOME HEATHER, AND SOME ROCKS

DEAR WHETSTONE,

I HOPE YOU ARE WELL. WE ARE ALL OK, UP
HERE IN ASGARD. I DON'T KNOW HOW MUCH ODIN
(ALLFATHER, CHIEF OF THE GODS, THE ONE-EYED
ONE, SPEAR SHAKER) IS LETTING YOU REMEMBER,
SO I WANTED TO WRITE TO YOU TO LET YOU KNOW
WHAT HAPPENED. I HOPE THIS LETTER REACHES
YOU — I'M NOT SURE HOW WELL IT WILL SURVIVE
THE TRIP.

ANYWAY, ODIN SENT ALL THE VIKINGS TO SLEEP,
AND I GOT A LIFT HOME ON SLEIPNIR. I THINK
ODIN KNOWS MORE ABOUT WHAT LOKI IS UP TO
THAN HE IS LETTING ON, BUT HE WOULDN'T TELL
ME ANYTHING. HE JUST KEEPS MAKING POINTED
COMMENTS ABOUT HOW HE HOPES 'SOMEONE' CAN
FIND THE HARP STRINGS AND RETURN THEM BEFORE
LOKI COMES BACK, AND THAT 'SOMEONE' SHOULD
PROBABLY THINK CAREFULLY ABOUT THE CLUES IN
THE RIDDLE.

Freyja (Goddess of Love) asked me what had happened to Loki, so I told her about him getting eaten by Nidhogg. After she finished laughing, she said he probably transformed himself into a rock or something so the dragon couldn't digest him. Freyja's never quite forgiven Loki for the time he tried to swap her for a barrel of enchanted mead.

Although being pooed out of a dragon sounds pretty disgusting, Loki's been through a lot worse, and somehow he always manages to come back. It also means that Loki will be able to find what's left of the harp in Niflheim. He'll still be after you to help him get the strings though.

Freyja also reckons Vali has been turned into a troll not a boulder, so he'll turn back into his normal (horrible) self and be able to move every time the sun goes down. You might want to sleep with one eye open. Freyja said his mum is going to go nuts when she finds out what happened.

Everyone was really impressed when they found out that we climbed down Yggdrasil.

Scold gave me a higher mark for my Animal Transformation exam. She said that even Akrid struggled to do it under pressure when she was a Class One. Flee and Flay are still out to get me, so nothing new there. They tried to put frogs in my boots yesterday, but Glinting-Fire caught them. They'll be cleaning armour for weeks!

I've got to get back to my Valkyrie training now. Scold said something about a big poetry contest in Valhalla coming up. Maybe I should ask Awfulrick if I can borrow his cup!

I'll try to keep in touch, although we're not supposed to meddle with humans (!)

Valhalla Forever!

Lotta

Trainee Valkyrie (still Class Three)

P.S. Broken Tooth misses you. I don't know why.

Continue reading for more fun in the Nine Worlds!

Here's a wordsearch full of 20 Viking words.
Can you find them all?

MIDGARD	LOTTA	WHETSTONE
KRUD	VALI	ASGARD
NIDHOGG	ODIN	YGGDRASIL
AWFULRICK	VIKING	RAGNAROK
LOKI	SCOLD	VALKYRIE

N	V	V	I	K	I	N	G	E	Y	G
W	H	E	T	S	T	O	N	E	G	E
L	S	V	U	C	G	H	D	R	G	S
O	V	C	L	S	I	U	A	T	D	I
T	K	L	O	D	I	N	W	Y	R	S
T	R	M	K	L	V	M	F	G	A	E
A	A	T	I	A	D	I	U	N	S	I
X	G	H	K	I	U	D	L	I	I	R
C	N	Z	O	W	K	G	R	D	L	Y
V	A	L	I	G	E	A	I	H	O	K
B	R	R	O	I	Y	R	C	O	T	L
P	O	K	R	U	D	D	K	G	S	A
Z	K	A	S	G	A	R	D	G	A	V

Viking Name Generator

Whetstone believes you haven't really made it until you're
Someone the Something. Give yourself a terrifying new
Viking name to strike fear into the hearts of your enemies.
If you need some inspiration use the ideas below.

First letter of your name:

Arne or Astrid	Nora or Njal
Bodil or Bjorn	Orm or Olga
Canute or Crag	Peg or Potar
Dagfin or Dagmar	Queil or Qual
Estrid or Erik	Ragnar or Revna
Frieda or Finn	Sven or Signe
Gunnar or Godrun	Tove or Torben
Harald or Hilda	Unn or Ulf
Ivar or Ingrid	Vidar or Vigdis
Jorunn or Jarl	Werda or Welk
Kari or Knud	Xannar or Xelhild
Liv or Leif	Yetta or Yorik
Marta or Magnus	Zara or Zeb

Month you were born:

January	Ferret or Sword
February	Raven or Shield
March	Boar or Kneecap
April	Horse or Finger
May	Wolf or Spear
June	Snake or Axe
July	Fox or Big Toe
August	Frog or Nose
September	Eagle or Skull
October	Bear or Tonsil
November	Flower or Knuckle
December	Dragon or Arrow

Day you were born:

1, 11, 21, 31	Biter or Hugger
2, 12, 21	Throttler or Tickler
3, 13, 23	Wrestler or Teaser
4, 14, 24	Squisher or Trainer
5, 15, 25	Grabber or Snuggler
6, 16, 26	Flinger or Tamer
7, 17, 27	Eater or Dancer
8, 18, 28	Stamper or Carrier
9, 19, 29	Mincer or Kisser
10, 20, 30	Stretcher or Cuddler

Put all the bits together to create your new name!
Cat Weldon's Viking name would be: *Crag the Frog Flinger*

Whoops. Lotta has made five big mistakes. Can you help correct her homework before Scold makes her clean out the stables again?

Valkyrie homework
By Brings-a-Lot-Of-Scrapes-And-Grazes

My favourite God is . . .
Odin because he doesn't let anyone stop him getting what he wants. Not even when it's a bad idea, like when he swapped one leg for a drink from the Well of Mimir to get more wisdom (although it might have been more wise to keep both as his depth perception is now a mess).

I'm pretty sure he has two legs, Lotta.

He also discovered maths by hanging upside down on Yggdrasil for nine days and nights, which must've been really boring and probably not worth it because if he didn't discover how to write, we wouldn't have to do this stupid homework.

We don't write with numbers.

He rides a horse called Susan who has eight legs and eats a lot of carrots. He also has two rabbits who fly around the Nine Worlds to bring him news and yet more wisdom. He can also do magic.

Are rabbits usually black and feathery?

Susan!?!

A world I would really like to visit is . . .
Muspell because I like skiing and they have lots of mountains. I am also really good at snowball fights so I could throw snowballs at Flee and Flay because they put my socks in the soup in Valhalla and now I have socks that smell like soup.

Muspell is full of fire and volcanos, not so good for skiing.

Lots of careless mistakes, Lotta. !
See me after class! – Scold.
PS: Also, please wash your socks.

Answers: eye, the Runes, Sleipnir, ravens, Jotunheim

There are 8 Viking runes hidden in the illustrations
throughout the book. Find them and use the translator below
to solve the riddle and unlock the first chapter of:

The Land of Lost Things

Whetstone wants to get to Helheim,
He will need this without fail.
Lotta's in big trouble,
And Loki's got one made of (toe) nails.
What am I?

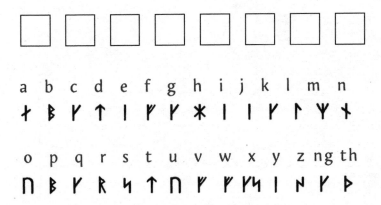

Chapter One

Deadman's Cove

'HEAVE!'

A rope was pressed into Whetstone's hands and he joined the Vikings of Krud struggling to drag the longboat into shore. Rain lashed down on the massive hairy men, their boots slipping on the pebbly beach. Inch by painful inch the boat crawled closer, fighting the wind and tide which seemed determined to keep it out at sea.

Whetstone's boots slithered on the wet rocks, nearly sending him tumbling. He gripped on as the rope burned against his hands. He didn't want to die in Deadman's Cove – it was far too predictable.

'COME ON, PUT YOUR BACKS INTO IT! WE'RE NEARLY THERE!' bellowed Awfulrick, Chief of the Vikings of Krud. The waves pounded, mixing sea spray with rain to create a cold, salty soup.

'We'll never make it,' panted Whetstone, scrubbing salt water out of his eyes with his sleeve. 'It's too rough.'

A man with arms like tree trunks waggled his eyebrows at him. 'That's right, keep positive.'

Whetstone pulled a face at Oresmiter, Awfulrick's second-in-command, then turned his attention back to the boat. You would have to be mad to go out in weather like this, although Vikings weren't generally known for their sensible decision making. They were much better known for feasting, fighting and falling asleep under the table.

It was thanks to Whetstone that the longboat had been noticed at all. He had been mooching along the cliffs when he spotted it far out at sea and clearly in trouble. Whetstone had been looking for a way out of Krud for weeks now, but strange weather had plagued the village. This was the first and only boat he had seen, the powerful wind and raging waves keeping everything else away from the shore.

Out at sea the ship looked tiny, tossed on the waves like a child's toy. But up-close it was *huge* and dangerous. Sleek sides lined with circular shields dipped low. A carved dragon figurehead snarled from the front.

With the crunch of wood on shingle the longboat reached the beach. The Vikings on board jumped off, joining the effort to pull the boat above the high-water mark. Whetstone's heart thudded in his chest: this boat was going to be his ticket out of Krud. All he had to do was talk his way onto the crew, prove himself useful, and . . .

'Get out of the way, weasel,' said Bragi, a young Viking with long-ish red hair and a big-ish nose. He gave Whetstone a shove, knocking him into a rockpool.

'WHETSTONE!' Oresmiter bellowed. 'Stop messing about. Get back to the village and tell Ethel to get a stew on for our visitors!'

'Fine.' Whetstone pulled a nosey crab out of his tunic and tossed it back into the water. Bits of slimy seaweed clung to his hands, he sneakily wiped them on Bragi's cloak. 'It's not as if fighting with wet wood and getting covered in splinters is my idea of a good time, anyway.'

Dodging out of the way as the boat was dragged up the beach, Whetstone started the long trudge towards the cliffs and back to Krud. He would find an opportunity to speak to the longboat crew later, when everyone was dry and in a better mood.

At the top of the cliffs, Whetstone's spine prickled. He turned to look down on the scene below him. The ship was safely on the beach now, the crew hurriedly unloading chests and other possessions as the rain bucketed down. But in the centre of the action, one man stood motionless, watching Whetstone. A man who had the bushiest red beard the boy had ever seen. Whetstone raised his hand in a wave, thinking it was never too early to make a good impression. Wind caught what was left of the ragged sail and an image of a sea serpent with gaping jaws billowed behind the man. Whetstone shivered and lowered his hand, pulling his cloak in tighter against the biting wind. He was sure he could still feel the eyes of the bearded man on him as he walked away.

Back at the Great Hall, Whetstone was met by great excitement. Fires had been built into infernos, fresh sawdust was spread on the floor and someone had even brought out the *fancy* plates – you know, the ones without the gnaw marks.

3

He nodded pointedly to Ethel and she dropped something scaly into the pot. The smell of fish rolled across the room catching in Whetstone's throat and making him cough.

The boy slid onto the bench furthest from the cauldron and tipped water out of his far-too-big boots, his mind still on the longboat and the strange, bearded man. The crew would be staying in Krud tonight, and tomorrow, Whetstone felt a jolt of excitement, he could be on his way to start his quest. He had wasted too much time waiting for Lotta already.

A few minutes later, just as Whetstone started to dry out, Awfulrick led the visitors into the Great Hall. There were about thirty men, all tired and wet. They dropped onto benches gratefully, puddles soon forming by their feet as rain and sea water dripped off their hair and clothes. The man with the red beard caught Whetstone's eye and winked.

'LOVELY DAY FOR A SAIL!' bellowed Awfulrick, slamming a cup of mead into the man's hand.

The man nodded, his beard bouncing up and down. 'We had fair winds until we got within sight of Krud. You must've done something to anger Thor.'

Awfulrick laughed. 'IT'S NOT THOR WE HAVE TO WORRY ABOUT.' He peered around the room. 'WHETSTONE! GET UP HERE AND TELL THEM WHAT YOU DID TO THAT DRAGON!'

Whetstone froze midway through wringing water out of his cloak. Awfulrick's magical cup bounced up and down on the Chief's shoulder like a demented metal parrot. It squeaked and then began to speak in a voice that sounded like a stuck

4

cutlery drawer:

> *Whetstone came to Krud with a feeling,*
> *That he just had to go stealing.*
> *He took this fine cup,*
> *But a colossal mix-up,*
> *Left him stranded in Asgard and reeling.*

> *A Valkyrie named Lotta was to blame,*
> *But Whetstone thought it was all a game.*
> *He was in for a shock,*
> *It was a long drop,*
> *To send him home once again.*

The crowd started to elbow each other and mutter. This story was a firm favourite with the Vikings of Krud.

> *Whetstone wanted to find Glory and Fame,*
> *To have us all knowing his name.*
> *So with Loki a deal he struck,*
> *To swap their freedom for Awfulrick's cup,*
> *But the Trickster was playing a game.*

> *Lotta agreed to help out with the quest,*
> *She wanted to prove that she was the best.*
> *They climbed down the tree,*
> *But things weren't easy,*
> *And they woke a dragon who wasn't impressed.*

Whetstone flattened his scruffy hair, he had always wanted to be famous. He just thought he would be a famous thief, not a Hero. A few of the Vikings started mouthing the words along with the cup.

The dragon was looking for food,
A tasty Valkyrie and Viking would do.
But instead the cup was dinner,
Till our Hero played a winner,
Beating the dragon and Loki, too!

The crowd burst into applause. Whetstone felt his heart speed up – if only it had been that easy. He still woke up in a sweat remembering Loki's dark eyes and twisted smile.

A large hand clamped around the neck of Whetstone's tunic, yanking him out of his memories and also off the bench. Oresmiter wheeled the boy to the front of the hall, his boots leaving long muddy streaks across the floor. The Vikings cheered.

Awfulrick stood outlined in front of the fireplace, the cup gleaming on his shoulder. 'THERE YOU ARE!'

Oresmiter released the boy. Whetstone stumbled, massaging his throat. The longboat crew eyed him with interest.

'SLAYER OF DRAGONS!'

'Actually, I didn't slay it and there was only one dragon,' Whetstone began modestly.

'SAVIOUR OF THE MAGIC CUP!'

'Well, yes, I suppose—'

'DEFEATER OF THIEVES!'

'I'm not sure, that—'

'FAVOURITE OF THE GODS!'

Whetstone tried not to grin as the Vikings of Krud started to stamp their feet and chant his name, 'Whet-stone, Whet-stone, WHET-STONE!'

'Don't forget that Odin, Chief of the Gods, decided Whetstone was officially a Hero and gave him a mighty quest!' the cup squeaked over the racket.

Whetstone made a grab for the cup who jumped onto Awfulrick's other shoulder. 'Shut up! You can't tell *anyone* about that,' the boy looked around in a panic.

'The way you got rid of that dragon was brilliant!' cried a short round Viking, wiping tears out of his eyes. 'Best thing to happen in Krud since Bjorn Brown Trousers was bitten on the bottom by a bear!'

The man from the longboat stroked his enormous beard. 'You sound like the sort of adventurous young man we could use on our crew.'

'YOU CAN'T HAVE HIM!' Awfulrick replied, squeezing Whetstone's shoulder in a move which was both comforting and stopped him leaving his side. 'HE'S STAYING IN KRUD. HE'S OUR GOOD LUCK CHARM.' Whetstone winced.

The cup jumped off Awfulrick's shoulder and landed in Whetstone's hands. It peered up at him with ruby eyes.

'Why won't you let me tell them how the adventure ends?' it complained. 'That was the best bit. You, me, Lotta, Odin, the riddle . . .'

Whetstone wiggled away from Awfulrick and wrapped his hands around the cup to muffle its voice. 'Shhh!'

The cup narrowed its eyes. 'But think of the poems I could make up! It's a quest worthy of great Heroes, Odin ordered you—' Whetstone tightened his hands around the cup's mouth but odd words still escaped, 'Skera harp— Dwarves— Loki—' Thinking the cup had finished, Whetstone relaxed his hands. 'SAVE THE NINE WORLDS!' the cup squealed loudly.

The Vikings gave a massive cheer. Cups of ale were thrown into the air. The dogs dozing in front of the fire woke up and started barking. Arrows were shot into the rafters knocking down dust, cobwebs and an unfortunate squirrel.

Whetstone slunk into a corner by the fireplace. 'You have to shut up! I *know* about the quest. I was there, remember? I have to return the cursed harp strings to the Dwarves before Loki finds them. But it's not exactly *easy*, is it?'

'No one ever said being a Hero was easy,' the cup replied tartly. 'Otherwise anyone could do it. Besides, I'm here to help you.'

'Yeah, thanks,' Whetstone grumbled.

'It's no use getting stroppy with me,' the cup pouted. 'I didn't steal the Skera Harp and curse your whole family. That was *mostly* Loki.'

'I *know*,' Whetstone hissed, squeezing the cup again. 'And

don't tell me that Loki will be back, because I know that too. He's a shapeshifter so being eaten by a dragon won't stop him for long.'

'He's just got to wait until the dragon poos him out,' the cup snickered.

'Poo!' yelled a tufty-haired Viking waving his mug in the air.

Whetstone huddled deeper into the shadows.

'You do remember the riddle, I gave you, don't you?' the cup asked, oblivious to Whetstone's discomfort. 'When I told you your fate?'

'You will seek to find, those who have been pulled apart,
A journey high and deep, into Yggdrasil's heart.'

Whetstone gritted his teeth. The cup could tell the fortune of anyone who held it, and that was the reason Loki made Whetstone take it in the first place. It had told Whetstone that his fate was to reunite his family, but Loki knew that by finding his parents, Whetstone would also reveal the location of the cursed harp strings, and Loki wanted the harp strings more than anything . . .

'One you will find below, in an iced locked land,
Still living but alone, for Hel holds him in her hand.'

'That's enough,' Whetstone gave the cup a little shake. 'I remember. It's not exactly something you forget.'

The cup fell silent. Whetstone unpeeled his hands. He had been holding it so tightly the pattern from the cup's sides was imprinted on his palms.

'I don't know why you've been hanging around here,' the cup complained. 'The sooner you start looking, the sooner you'll find them. Then I can make up more fantastic poems about your valiant quest!'

'I've been busy planning stuff! The Nine Worlds are depending on me, it's a lot of pressure.' Whetstone sighed, his shoulders slumping. 'And I've been waiting for Lotta. She promised to come back and help me, but I haven't heard from her in weeks.'

'Of course not,' the cup replied. 'She's busy with Valkyrie business. You need to get on with things on your own. Have you figured out where the first harp string is yet?'

'It must be in Helheim, that's where Hel lives,' Whetstone muttered. 'But how do I get there? I can't even get out of Krud.'

'Not with that attitude,' the cup replied primly. 'Helheim is the Land of Lost Things. So you should, you know . . . get lost!' The cup jumped onto a nearby table and vanished among the Vikings.

Needing some fresh air, Whetstone sidled to the door to the Great Hall and slipped out. Dark clouds hung above him filling the sky with the promise of yet more rain. Whetstone pushed his hood down, enjoying the novel sensation of being outside and dry at the same time.

His feet unthinkingly followed the familiar path towards

the field outside the village. He never asked for any of this. If it hadn't been for Loki and his schemes, Whetstone would have had a normal life with a normal parents and normal friends.

The boy squelched his way along the rutted path. He made this journey at least once a day, visiting a boy sized boulder which was all that was left of Loki's son, Vali. Loki had transformed him into a rock when Vali finally defied him. Although Whetstone and Vali had never been friends, Whetstone found it reassuring to visit what was left of him. It helped remind him that his adventures weren't some sort of mad dream.

Whetstone stuck his hands in his pockets, fingers feeling for the crumpled *Guide to the Nine Worlds*. It was the last thing Lotta had given him before returning to Asgard. Lotta had got in a lot of trouble for accidentally bringing Whetstone to the World of the Gods instead of a dead Hero like she was supposed to. It was only when Whetstone had proved his worth by getting rid of the dragon that she was able to continue with her Valkyrie training.

Whetstone pulled the tattered pages out of his pocket. Another fragment of paper was stuck to the front cover.

I'm sorry – stuck in Asgard. Don't start the quest without me!
Lotta

Lotta had sent him that note three weeks ago. Since then, there had been nothing. *Don't start the quest without me.* It was all very well Lotta saying that, but he was the one left kicking his heels in Krud waiting for her to show up. He couldn't exactly march up to Asgard and find her himself. He smiled, imagining the scene. 'Excuse me, Odin, Chief of the Gods, Spear Shaker, One Eyed Thunderer, is Lotta the Valkyrie in? I need to talk to her.' Whetstone sniggered, picturing the God's expression.

Whetstone rounded the bend, following the path of churned mud to Vali's boulder. Sometimes when the light was right, you could almost see a face in the rock. Lotta had said that Vali had been transformed into a troll, not just an ordinary boulder, so when the sun went down he should be able to move, but he would turn back into stone when the sun rose. Except the boulder hadn't moved an inch so far. Maybe he was just a boulder after all.

Whetstone glanced up, expecting to see the familiar shape outlined against the horizon.

His feet stopped. His knees locked.

The boulder was gone.

Whetstone spun on the spot, his heart hammering. He was definitely in the right place, there was even a patch of dead grass where the boulder had been. Vali had gone but something was left, burnt into the grass in tall black letters.

He'S ComINg

Authors Note

I have had enormous fun in writing Whetstone and Lotta's story. The world of Norse Mythology is rich and complex, but it is also incomplete and, in some places, completely bonkers.

The backbone of Norse mythology is a giant tree whose roots and branches support Nine Worlds. This is a fantastic idea, but how would it actually work for the inhabitants? If we are all in the tree, could I, if I had sufficient tree climbing skills, climb from one world to another? But then, if humans can cross between worlds, why not monsters? And what if someone with an eye for mischief saw this as an opportunity to cause trouble and seize power?

Odin, Freyja and the other Gods and Goddesses Whetstone encounters are all real figures within Norse Mythology. Of them, Loki is the most curious. Not technically a God but a shapeshifting Fire Giant. While everyone else is brave and straightforward, Loki is more . . . complicated. He saves the Gods and endangers them seemingly at random and his actions will ultimately bring about the downfall of the Gods and Giants. Despite this, the Gods wilfully tolerate his behaviour until it is far too late.

Knowledge of the Gods own downfall colours all the stories within Norse mythology. They know from the beginning how everything will end and although this can be delayed, it will still come to pass. Interestingly the Gods are not immortal, they can and do die. It was felt that you cannot be truly heroic if you cannot risk everything. Odin builds his ghostly army in Valhalla not because he believes he can beat the Frost Giants, but simply to go out in a final blaze of glory. Valhalla is the ultimate afterparty, but only those who had done enough to catch Odin's (one remaining) eye would be invited to join.

As for Odin's elite warriors, the Valkyries, their origins are unclear. Are they born or made? In some stories they start off as the daughters of noble families, in others they are bloodthirsty spirits luring fighters to their deaths. As well as being the god of Wisdom, Odin was also the God of battle frenzy. My Valkyries are made of this battle frenzy and originate from battles across Europe, Asia, North Africa and North America. All places it is known that the Vikings travelled to. Out of great battles, come great Valkyries.

Although the Vikings would have been familiar with lots of different characters and stories from Norse mythology, not many details have survived the last thousand years to reach us today. These remaining stories inspired *How to be a Hero*, which takes place in the spaces between the myths.

Acknowledgements

This is the bit of the book where I get to thank all the people who helped me write it. By that, I don't mean they sat next to me and pointed out my typos, although that might have been helpful . . .

Firstly, thank you to my wonderful husband, Steve (who thinks I should just say it was all down to him), and our gorgeous children, Georgia and Immie. Thank you for letting me shut myself away for days on end to actually write this story (and for not letting me chuck it all in the bin when it all got too much). Thank you to my mum for filling my childhood with books, and for providing endless support.

Publishing is a strange and confusing world and I have to thank my fabulous agent, Alice Williams, for holding my hand through the tricky bits. I want to thank the whole team at Macmillan for showing such support and enthusiasm for Whetstone and Lotta, especially Lucy Pearce, Rachel Petty, Sim Sandhu, and Sabina Maharjan. You are all wonderful people and this book would look very different without you!

A big thank you to Katie Kear for bringing the characters and worlds to life through her fabulous illustrations. I especially love all the facial expressions!

Thank you to my friends and family for supporting me. Especially Becky Sorapure for being the first person to read (and, she says, enjoy) this book, and Kelly Wilmer for her willingness to listen to me endlessly banging on about all the weird bits in Norse Mythology.

A final thank you goes to Mai Black and everyone at her Thursday evening Writing Group for reminding me about grammar and punctuation, which as a former English teacher I obviously already know all about, and more importantly for keeping me supplied in biscuits and enthusiasm.

About the Author

Cat Weldon writes funny books for children and is a little bit obsessed with Vikings. With an MA in Scriptwriting, and a background in children's theatre, Cat has also worked as an English and Drama teacher – and in lots of other jobs where she can talk while waving her hands around wildly.

Cat Weldon now lives in East Anglia with her husband, daughters, and collection of delinquent chickens.

Although she has a favourite cup, it has never once recited poetry to her.

About the Illustrator

Katie Kear is a British illustrator and has been creating artwork for as long as she can remember.

Katie has an illustration degree from the University of Gloucestershire and has worked with publishers including Pan Macmillan, Penguin Australia, Andersen Press and Hachette. She is always on the hunt for brilliant stories to illustrate.

In her spare time she loves drawing, adventures in nature, chocolate, stationery, the smell of cherries and finding new inspirational artists!